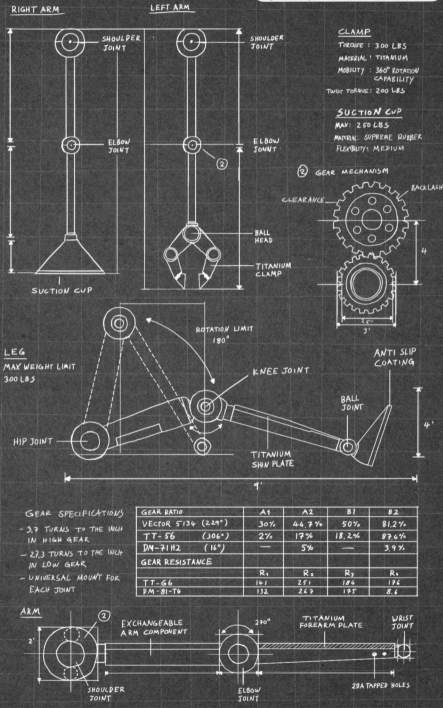

ROBOTS RULE!

THE JUNKYARD BOT

THE JUNKYARD BOT

C. J. Richards

Illustrated by Goro Fujita

Houghton Mifflin Harcourt
Boston   New York

With special thanks to Brandon Robshaw

www.hmhco.com

Book design by Elizabeth Tardiff
Text set in Adobe Garamond

Library of Congress Cataloging-in-Publication Data is available.
LCCN 2013042821

Manufactured in the United States of America
DOC 10 9 8 7 6 5 4 3 2 1
4500495841

To my dad:
For all the stories
we wrote on hotel stationery
and recorded on cassette
and told on car trips,
this one's for you

1

A voice boomed in the darkness.

"GET UP, YOU LAZY SLOB!"

George Gearing opened his eyes and, still half asleep, lifted his head from the pillow. "Who? What?"

"ON THE FLOOR AND GIVE ME TWENTY, PEA BRAIN!"

George rubbed his eyes. The light that filled the room was blinding.

"OUT OF BED, MISTER!"

George had tried to reprogram his Sergeant Wake-Me-Up clock to speak in a gentle, feminine voice, but something must have gone wrong. It had reverted to factory settings.

"I WON'T TELL YOU AGAIN!"

The clock started blaring a recording of a bugle from across the room on George's desk. The windows rattled with the sound.

George plugged his fingers into his ears. "Jackbot!" he shouted.

The door opened, and three feet of scrap and spare parts rattled into the room on wobbly legs. Jackbot's head tilted toward the bed, and his green eyes flashed.

"Yes, George," he said in his expressionless mechanical voice.

"Shut that thing up, would you?"

"Yes, George."

"DON'T MAKE ME COME OVER THERE!"

Jackbot scooped up the alarm clock in his right pincer and placed it on the floor. He raised a metal foot, motors whirring.

"OF ALL THE GOOD-FOR-NOTHING, INSUBORDINATE—"

Crunch.

Bits of metal and plastic flew across the room. The

bugle gave a final despairing wail, then fell silent.

"That was—uh—a little extreme," George said. But it was no use blaming Jackbot. Robots just do what they are told.

George sat up in bed. "Could I have my glasses?"

Jackbot trotted forward and handed George his glasses using his left-hand suction grip.

"Thanks."

"Yes, George."

George put his glasses on, and the mess of his room swam into focus. Transistor boards and loose wires littered the floor beside an open copy of Professor Droid's book *Advanced Robotics*. George had been working late

into the night on a new baseball drive for Jackbot. If he could just program him to catch, their games would be a lot more fun.

George climbed out of bed and picked his way through the debris to his closet to find some clothes. A couple of old photos had fallen off the door, so he carefully stuck them back up. One, from last summer, showed Jackbot and George fishing at the lake. The other showed Jackbot teetering precariously on George's skateboard. George grinned, recalling the day Jackbot's balance sensors had failed on a steep bit of sidewalk by the neighbor's front yard.

"You remember the day you flattened Mrs. Glitch's rosebush, Jackbot?" he said. "I thought she was going to blow a gasket!"

"Yes, George," said Jackbot.

George smoothed his wiry brown hair in the mirror, pulled on his pants and a shirt, and scooped up Jackbot to carry him downstairs. He'd been working on a stairs program for ages, but it was surprisingly complicated.

Uncle Otto was wearing his usual dingy plaid work shirt and jeans, his barrel-chested frame balanced on a rickety chair as he sat at the kitchen table. He didn't raise his head when George walked in. He was stabbing at a battered tablet with oily fingers while munching on a piece of brown toast. The crumbs tumbled down into his half-grown beard. A greasy carburetor that he'd been working on sat in the middle of the table.

"Morning, Uncle Otto," George said. He glanced over his uncle's shoulder and saw he was scrolling through an article about cars. Big surprise.

His uncle made a sort of grunting noise, which George knew was as close to a hello as he was likely to get.

George sat at the table and put Jackbot down on the floor beside him. Mr. Egg, the cook-bot, trundled over on its squeaking caster wheels.

"Good-morning-sir," it said in its flat, tinny voice. "Would-you-like-a-piece-of-toast."

"Sure," George said.

Mr. Egg inserted a slice of bread into the slot in its chest and pressed its nose. A low humming noise started up, and the toast slot glowed red.

"Would-you-like-a-glass-of-juice."

"Sounds good," said George—then he had to act fast as Mr. Egg held the glass directly above the boy's lap. George just managed to grab it before Mr. Egg let it fall. *One benefit of having Mr. Egg in the kitchen,* he thought. *It's good for the reflexes!*

George sipped his juice and watched the sunlight reflecting off the metal surfaces of Jackbot, Mr. Egg, and Scrubby, the dishwasher-bot. They were shabby robots, but the light pretty much brightened them up all the same. "Nice day," George murmured absent-mindedly.

Otto flipped over a page on the screen of his tablet. "Get me another coffee," he said, holding out his cup to Mr. Egg. As the robot's metal pincer grasped the cup, smoke began to pour out from the grill in its chest.

"Toast-is-ready," said the robot. It slid a piece of blackened toast onto the plate in front of George.

"Um," said George, wondering if it was even edible.

"Coffee-is-ready," said the cook-bot.

It dropped the cup of scalding coffee into Uncle Otto's lap.

"Yow!" yelped Otto, leaping to his feet. He tore off his steaming pants and stood fuming in his boxer shorts. George saw that they were decorated with little race-cars and tried not to snicker. "You hunk of metal, you could've put me in the hospital!" yelled Otto.

"Are you okay?" asked George, trying to look serious.

"I'll survive, no thanks to you! If we have to live our lives surrounded by these thinking tin cans, can you at least make them work properly?"

George wanted to explain that their robots needed more than just a few replacement parts. They weren't like cars, which could have their spark plugs changed and be given a drink of oil. The house-bots needed complete reprogramming—a system overhaul—to get rid of all the bugs making them malfunction. But something told him that his uncle wasn't in the mood for excuses. He didn't like the bots at the best of times. So George went silent, staring down at his burnt toast.

"Every robot in this house is a useless pile of bolts!" Otto railed on. "The gardener-bot drowns all the plants, and the dishwasher-bot leaves crusty stains on the dishes!"

"Its name is Scrubby," George began. "And it just needs—"

"Whatever!" Otto growled. He grabbed his grease-stained tool bag and made for the door. "I don't have time for this nonsense. I'm going to work."

"Uh, Uncle Otto?"

"What now?"

"You're not wearing any pants."

Otto looked down at his bare legs. He seemed to be trying to think of something to say, but thought better of it and stomped off upstairs. George heard him angrily tearing around his room. A minute later Otto stomped back down again, wearing another pair of grimy jeans.

He looked at George with narrowed eyes and said, "Not a word." Then he walked through the front door and slammed it behind him.

"Hey, Jackbot?" George said after his uncle was gone.

"Yes, George."

"Could you make some toast? I mean, a piece I could actually eat."

"Yes, George."

Jackbot took a slice of bread and heated it with his soldering attachment until it was golden brown. Then he added a layer of butter and served the toast to George on a plate. He'd even singed a smiley face into it.

"Oh, wow—thanks!" George said, even though he'd programmed Jackbot to do it.

As George bit into his toast, he picked up the tablet Uncle Otto had left behind. George scrolled back to see the day's news. There was the usual sort of stuff: Mayor

Buffer was promising to be tough on cybercrime, the workers who programmed the street-cleaning robots were threatening to go on strike, and a team of scientists had genetically engineered an orange as big as a pumpkin.

Then George's eyes fell on an ad. It showed the gleaming towers of a building that George, and everyone else in Terabyte Heights, knew very well: TinkerTech Enterprises HQ. George touched the ad with the tip of his finger, and it came to life. The main door of the building opened and a man came out. He walked right up close until his head filled the screen. He had black hair with a touch of gray at the temples; a square, handsome face; and a cleft in his chin.

"Hi, there," the man said, his voice deep and rich. "Are you smart? Under eighteen? And are you *dying* to work in the exciting field of cutting-edge robotics? If so, this might be your lucky day. My name is Charles Micron, and I'm the deputy head of Robotics at TinkerTech. We're looking for a very special young person to be our newest apprentice. If you want to work at the greatest

company in the world and you think you've got what it takes, don't wait—apply today."

How cool would that be? George thought. He couldn't think of anything he'd rather do than work with his hero, Dr. Micron, and learn how to design even more amazing robots. *"He may only be eleven years old,"* George imagined Dr. Micron announcing to the press, *"but my new*

apprentice, George Gearing, has an instinctive understand-ing of robots . . ."

TinkerTech was the biggest company in town. It was the reason Terabyte Heights existed in the first place. Way back before George was born, a young genius named Professor A. I. Droid had used his savings to buy a piece of virtually unpopulated land in the middle of nowhere and start a company. He recruited the best technological brains from the entire world to work for him, luring them with the promise of total freedom to invent anything and everything they could dream of. As the company grew, so did Terabyte Heights. The employees and their families needed places to live, and so grocery stores, schools, and shops of all kinds popped up to serve them. Droid was definitely one of George's heros, but it was his second-in-command, the brilliant Dr. Micron, that George idolized the most. George wanted more than anything to be just like him when he grew up.

Micron's smiling face remained on the screen after the

ad ended. Then it faded away. The door of TinkerTech HQ reopened and Dr. Micron emerged exactly as before. "Hi, there," he said. "Are you smart? Under eighteen . . ."

George sighed and turned the tablet off. He had to finish his breakfast and get ready for school. What was the point of daydreaming? He'd never get the apprenticeship. He was too young, for one thing: they said "under eighteen," but that didn't mean *ten and a half.* And even if he were older, what chance would he have? Almost anyone who applied would have better connections and more experience than he did. Just about every kid in George's school had at least one parent who worked at TinkerTech. All George had was Uncle Otto and his grimy junkyard. His parents had worked for TinkerTech, but just in the data-filing department. And that was a long time ago.

The doorbell rang, and George crammed the rest of his breakfast into his mouth as he headed into the front hall. He flicked the transparency switch, and the door gave him a view of his elderly neighbor standing on the doorstep, her face crinkled with anxiety. George opened the door. "Hi, Mrs. Glitch."

"I'm so sorry to trouble you, George. It's Lenny. He's acting up again."

"What's he doing this time?" George asked.

Lenny was Mrs. Glitch's ancient helper-bot, and its circuits had gone out of date ten years ago. George did his best to patch up the robot, but he'd seen vacuum cleaners with more complex wiring.

"He's hanging from a tree outside my house, and he won't come down."

"Huh," said George thoughtfully. "Probably an issue with the geotropic sensors. Either that or he thinks he's a bat." He checked his watch. "I've got a few minutes before the school bus comes. I'll get my gear."

"That's really sweet of you," Mrs. Glitch said, patting George on the shoulder.

George ran upstairs to grab his trusty tool bag. He didn't get many chances to put his talents to use, so he liked to help out his neighbors whenever their robots went on the fritz. Most of them couldn't afford the latest helper-bots, so he patched up their ancient ones with scrap. Needless to say, he was very popular with the retirees on the block. They were always offering him hard candies and inviting him to dinner at four o'clock.

"You coming, Jackbot?" George asked as he clumped down the last stair.

"Yes, George," said Jackbot, wobbling after him.

As they were crossing the road, George heard a metallic clatter. He turned around and saw that a screwdriver had fallen from his bag. "Hey, Jackbot, can you get that for me?" he said.

"Yes, George," Jackbot said, and he ambled back into the middle of the street—just as a huge silver car came surging around the corner. It wasn't slowing down.

"Jackbot! Look out!" yelled George.

"Yes, Ge—"

CRASH!

With a sound like a hundred hammers on a tin can, the car smashed into Jackbot, sending him high into the air. The robot turned three somersaults and landed on his back with a sickening crunch. One of his arms skidded across the pavement, sparks flying.

"Eerrghrifipfipfip! *ZUMZUM! Plip. WHIRRR . . . splosh,*" said Jackbot.

"Jackbot!" George shouted in horror. "Are you okay?"

Jackbot's trailing wires fizzed and crackled, and the green light behind his eyes flickered.

Then his head fell off.

2

George was frozen with shock. He stood star-ing at Jackbot's head, then at his body, then at his head again.

"Good heavens!" said Mrs. Glitch. "Oh, George, are you all right?"

The back door of the silver car opened, and a girl jumped out and headed over to what was left of Jackbot. She had messy white-blond hair, and her pale complexion suggested that she got out of the house even less than George did. She looked about George's age, but oddly, he'd never seen her at school.

The girl whistled. "Man, that pile of pistons really

got some distance!" she said, staring down at Jackbot as he lay smoking at the side of the road.

A painful lump grew in the back of George's throat as he walked toward his robot friend.

The girl must have seen the stricken look on George's face as he approached. Her expression softened. "Hey, now, don't get your underwear in a twist. It's just a robot. We'll stick its head back on, tighten a few screws, and it'll be as good as new, right?"

George crouched next to Jackbot and shook his head hopelessly. "Are you kidding? His exoskeleton is a mess—the circuitry inside must be fried. It took me months to collect and repair these parts. There's no way I'll find the same ones again. Even if I could fix him, he'd never be the same."

The girl's face lit up in a smile. "Well! It's your lucky day, my friend," she said. Then, looking down at Jackbot, she added, "Well, maybe not your *luckiest* day. But still! If it's robot junk you want, I know just the place. My father's workshop has everything—if you can't find what you need there, it doesn't exist!"

A tiny diode of hope flickered in George's heart. "You don't even know my name. You'd really do that for me?"

"It was my car that wrecked your robot," said the girl. "It's the least I can do. C'mon, jump in!"

"Go on, George," said Mrs. Glitch, wringing her hands on the sidewalk. "It's worth a try. If anyone can fix him, it's you!"

George nodded uncertainly. He gathered all of Jackbot's pieces in his arms and followed the girl to the car door.

"Warning!" the car said the moment George set foot inside. "I am not authorized to carry unregistered passengers. You are required at home for scheduled classes."

"Can it, car!" the girl said. "I'm a human being and you're a hunk of metal, so I get to call the shots around here. Get in," she said to George.

George climbed into the back of the car and sank into a soft seat. The windows, tinted from the outside, had screens that flashed a variety of channels, weather reports, and movies. The girl hopped in beside him. George scanned the cold metal pieces of Jackbot sadly.

"Nice car," said George, absently.

"Thank you," said the car.

"Just take us home," the girl said. She pressed a button and turned the windows into regular see-through glass.

"Fasten your seat belts, please," said the car. After they'd done so, it set off smoothly down the road.

"My name's Anne," said the girl.

"I'm George," he replied. "And this is . . . was . . .

Jackbot." George's voice trembled as he said his friend's name.

He saw a flash of confusion on the girl's face. "Hey, if we can't fix him, we'll get you a new one. I mean, he *does* look a little . . . um . . . old."

That's not the point! George wanted to say. *A new bot wouldn't be the same.*

Silence fell over the car, until George decided to break it. "So—how come I've never seen you before? Don't you go to school around here?"

"Nah, I'm homeschooled," Anne said. "I kind of got into a few scrapes at my old schools, so my dad decided it was better if I was educated at home."

"So you don't have to go to school?" George asked, envious. "That must be amazing!"

"It's boring, mostly," said Anne. She was quiet for a moment. "Don't you like your school?"

George thought of all the kids who looked down on him for not having the latest cool gadgets and all the other kids who were just too scared of the bullies to be his friend. He shook his head. "Not really, no."

George watched the town pass by for a while, and hoped Anne's house wasn't much farther. Jackbot's head was faintly warm. There was still a chance—a slim chance—that the robot's brain circuitry and memory could be saved, if the capacitors weren't completely burned up.

"So—is your father some kind of mechanic?" George asked. "Since he has this amazing workshop."

"Well, yeah, you could say that," said Anne. "What about you? What do your parents do?"

"I live with my uncle," said George. "He owns Otto's Grotto—the parts yard across town. My parents died when I was little."

Anne bit her lip. "I'm really sorry to hear that," she said softly.

"It's no big deal—I mean, it *was* a big deal, but you know, it's not your fault," George said, and he could have kicked himself for sounding so dumb. He pressed his mouth shut and vowed not to talk for the rest of the trip.

Nervously, George let his hand drift into his right

pocket. His fingers closed around his lucky marble and rolled it around. It was an old habit—sometimes it was the only thing that could calm him down when he was upset. He carried the marble everywhere. His dad had given it to him when he was three years old, a few days before the crash. Besides Jackbot, it was the most precious thing he owned.

George stared out the window at the town robots going about their business. A huge automated garbage collector emptied trash cans into its metal jaws and crunched the contents. Long-armed window-cleaning robots telescoped their wipers to reach the highest windows. Other robots were picking up litter from the sidewalk and mowing lawns. At the corner of each block were tall steel towers with glowing balls at the top: the power hubs. The robots stayed fully charged just by working near the hubs. No plugs or wires were needed. It was another one of TinkerTech's brilliant inventions.

These robots were all working just fine, George thought sadly. And if one of them broke down, nobody would shed any tears. They were just machines, doing jobs. They weren't anyone's *friends*.

The car stopped as a traffic robot stepped into the road and held out a metal hand, eyes flashing red.

The delay was torture. "Can we please hurry?" George said.

Anne nodded. "Did you hear that, car?" she said. "Step on it!"

The traffic robot's eyes turned green and it stepped aside. The car gave a burst of speed. Houses and streets whizzed by.

Soon they were traveling uphill to the most exclusive part of town, Binary Bluffs. Huge mansions with sculpted trees and wide lawns lined the roadside. The car stopped outside the biggest mansion of all, right at the top of Terabyte Heights, overlooking the whole town.

"Nice house," George said as he got out of the car, carrying Jackbot.

"Thank you," said a loud voice.

George jumped in surprise. "Did the house just talk to me?"

"Yup," said Anne. "Don't flatter it, though—it's already got an ego problem."

The garage doors slid noiselessly apart and the silver car parked itself. Then the front door swung open to reveal a huge entrance hall with a black-and-white tiled floor. The translucent walls glowed with light, and within them George could see streams of data cascading down in multicolored patterns, like living wallpaper. A maid-bot in a white apron was cleaning a shelf of knick-knacks with a feather-duster arm attachment.

"Come in! Come in!" said the house in a voice that sounded like a short-tempered kindergarten teacher. "Shut the door! You're letting the flies in."

George stepped inside and looked unsuccessfully for the speakers. The voice just seemed to be coming from the air all around him.

"Identify this unauthorized person!" commanded the house.

"House, meet George," said Anne. "George, this is my annoying house."

"Wipe your feet!" said the house.

George did as he was told.

Somewhere, a dog barked. A second later, a pet-bot came bounding down the stairs, its antenna tail wagging and yellow eyes flashing. It jumped up at Anne to welcome her, its silicon tongue lolling out of its mouth.

"Hi, Sparky!" Anne said. "This is my dog," she said to George. "Isn't he sweet?"

The dog ran around in circles and farted. It smelled like exhaust.

"Yeah, very sweet," George said.

"Sorry, he does that when he gets excited."

"It's okay, really," said George anxiously. "But we need to get to the workshop as fast as possible. Jackbot's getting cold—"

"Sure!" said Anne. "Right away. House, we're going to the workshop."

"Unacceptable!" the house said. "Math lessons will commence in precisely two minutes and fifteen seconds. Make your way to the classroom for quadratic equations!"

George looked at Anne. "So . . . when you said you were homeschooled, you were—"

"Dead serious," said Anne. "The house is literally my teacher. Lame, right? Come on."

"I shall inform your father of this insubordination!" said the house.

"You do that. Come on, George."

"Won't you get into trouble?" George asked as he scrambled after her down the long hallway.

Anne shrugged. "Don't worry about it. It's not a problem."

George gazed at the huge framed photographs that

lined the walls. In all of them the same distinguished, silver-haired man could be seen shaking hands with politicians, smiling next to movie stars, sharing a joke with famous millionaires.

"Wait a minute," George said, staring at a picture of a man in a pizza restaurant with the entire Terabyte Heights baseball team. "That's—that's Professor Droid, isn't it? The head of TinkerTech?"

"Yep," said Anne. She blushed slightly. "That's my dad."

George's jaw dropped. He could only think of only one word to say. "Wow!" Then he chuckled. "So your name is Anne Droid."

"What's so funny?" she said.

George tried not to smile. "Y'know. Anne Droid? Android."

Anne rolled her eyes.

"I guess you've heard that before, right?"

"Just once or twice," said Anne. "C'mon, let's go!" She led him through a maze of passages until they came to a massive steel door with a sign that said AUTHORIZED PERSONNEL ONLY.

Tiny silver light bulbs set into the door's surface lit up at their approach. "Identify," the door said.

Anne took a palm-size device from her pocket. It was a Series 7 Personal SmartTablet—George knew from his tech magazines that it wasn't coming out for another couple of months.

Anne touched the tablet, and a voice spoke up—a man's voice, precise and authoritative. "Open up, door, or I'll replace you with a bead curtain!"

"That's your dad's voice!" whispered George.

"Yep. I recorded it when he wasn't looking. Not very high-tech, but hey, it works!"

"Welcome, Professor," said the door, sliding open without a sound. Behind it was a square room, which turned out to be the chamber of an elevator. It had mirrored glass sides.

"After you," said Anne.

The door slid shut behind them. George felt a slight

jolt, then a sensation of very fast movement. Only the elevator wasn't going *up*—it was traveling sideways.

"What *is* this?" George asked.

"Oh, it's just part of my dad's personal transport system," Anne said as casually as if she were discussing her father's choice of carpet. "It connects our house with the TinkerTech workshop. Saves time."

"Do you hear that, Jackbot?" said George. "We're going to the *TinkerTech workshop!* Hang in there, buddy."

In the mirror, he caught Anne looking at him strangely again. Most people didn't speak to their robots the way he did.

Seconds later the transport chamber came to a halt. The doors opened, and George gazed out in wonder. The workshop stretched as far as the eye could see. Robots worked at benches, making more robots. Banks of computer screens displayed constantly changing charts and graphics and calculations. Spare robot parts hung on the walls: legs and arms of all sizes, blinking circuit boards, electronic brains bristling with fiber-optic cables.

"Well, what are you waiting for? Help yourself!" said Anne.

George was speechless. He placed Jackbot on a table and grabbed a robotic spinal column from one of the shelves. "This'll get his head and body reconnected," he said, getting his mind focused on the task. "I'll need a screwdriver—and a soldering iron."

Anne handed George a soldering iron from one of the benches and watched as he removed Jackbot's old twisted spinal column and fitted the new one into place.

"Now I'm going to need a new circuit board for the body, some self-charging batteries—that way, he won't need the power-hubs when we're off on fishing trips."

Soon, George was in the zone. Everything other than the work in his hands faded away, and his thoughts became a flurry of designs and calculations. He ran around the workshop snatching up the necessary equipment. In just a few minutes, he had the circuits replaced and the new power source up and running. George's heart leaped as Jackbot's eyes came to life with a feeble glow.

"Jackbot! Can you hear me? Can you speak?"

Jackbot gave no sign that he had heard.

"Just a second," George said. "I need to look inside your head, okay?"

He pried off the back of Jackbot's head plate and peered inside. His heart sank as he saw the rat's nest of cards, chips, boards, and wiring that Jackbot's brain had become.

"I don't know how I'm going to fix this," George said, breathing hard. "Do you?"

Anne shook her head. "Robotics isn't exactly my thing. I have, um, *other* skills."

"But—you're Professor Droid's daughter. You must have some idea!"

"It's all just nuts and bolts to me," Anne said. "But hey—I saw the way that old lady looked at you. Like you were some kind of genius. So c'mon, Robot Boy, let's see what you've got!"

"Yeah," George said, nodding. Jackbot's brain was beyond repair, but with all the parts in the workshop, he could build a new one. "I can do this," he muttered. Anne gave him a thumbs-up.

George started walking up and down the workshop, grabbing things that caught his eye. He felt giddy, like a kid in a candy shop. As he added one piece after another to the pile on the table, a plan began to form in his mind. A completely crazy plan—but one that he thought just might work.

He came back and stared at Jackbot and his towering pile of parts. "Look at this," he said to Anne. "I've got a positronic memory drive and a cognition simulator drive. If I link those together and rewrite their programming using human response simulation commands, and then replace the standard processors with these new microchips . . ."

George rattled on as he worked, doing things that he'd dreamed of doing but had never had the equipment or the parts to create. The state-of-the-art chips were so tiny that he could fit a lot more into Jackbot's central processing unit. The latest tech was all virtually connected—linking electromagnetically—so he didn't need to sort through a tangle of wiring. He added everything he could think of: a voice intonation program, an impulse generator, a vocabulary extension unit—all custom-built using designs George had been working on for years but never had the parts to try out until now. For good measure, he threw in a dancing expertise program. Jackbot would be great at parties.

"Done!" said George.

"Did it work?" asked Anne.

"Only one way to find out," said George. "Let's boot him up."

He reached for the reset switch under Jackbot's chin, but paused.

"What is it?" said Anne.

George narrowed his eyes. He'd just had an idea. Possibly a stupid one, but it was worth a try.

"I don't want to rush you, but I'll be given extra math homework by my house if we don't get back soon," said Anne.

"Can you get a light in here?" said George, opening Jackbot's head again.

Anne took a micro-flashlight and shone it into the cavity. "Did you miss something?" she said.

George put on a pair of magnifying spectacles. "No," he said. "See, normally a robot's brain function filters incoming signals—sounds, sights, smells—through the circuits, and produces an output."

"Okay . . ."

"It's been that way since before Terabyte Heights was on the map," said George. "But what if we loop the signal, sending the outputs back into the processor, refining the robot's response?"

Anne raised an eyebrow at George. "Honestly? I have no idea what you're talking about. But it sounds like you do." She saw George's doubtful expression and slapped him on the back. "Come on! You'll never know until you try!"

George worked delicately on the looping circuit, then scanned the desk for a high-grade capacitor to handle the added processing power. "If this works," he said, "Jackbot will be thousands of times more advanced than before."

"And if it doesn't?" said Anne.

George closed the cavity. "Then I've just wasted a lot of your dad's stuff."

Anne didn't understand very much of what George was saying, but then only a few people would. George was pretty sure no one had ever tried this before. His fingers found the reset switch.

"Here goes nothing," George said, his stomach bubbling with nervous energy. He flicked the switch.

For one tense moment, nothing happened.

Then nothing happened for another tense moment.

But at the end of the third tense moment, Jackbot's eyes lit up brightly. He turned his head toward George. "Hello, George," he said. "You look like you've seen a ghost! What's going on?"

George's whole body filled with relief and happiness. He felt ready to float off the floor like a balloon. "Jackbot! You're alive!"

"Nice job, Robot Boy," said Anne, and gave George a high-five.

"Oh, yes, I'm alive," Jackbot said. "Living. Animated. Full of life, exuberance, and vitality."

George stared at Jackbot. "That vocabulary extension unit certainly seems to have worked!"

"Why, thank you!" Jackbot said. "Squid! Handbag! Ooze! Dinosaur! Mountain! Puddle! Negotiate! Nevertheless! Ice cream! Cathedral! Glory! Elephant! Pyramid! Supercalifragilisticexpialidocious!"

"And just what is going on here?" said a deep voice.

George spun around to see Dr. Charles Micron

standing in the doorway, his arms folded. George had always wanted to meet his hero. But his hero did not look very happy to see him.

"It's all right!" said Anne. "I brought him here. My car hit this robot—and I thought it was only fair to get it fixed. I'm sure my dad won't mind." Anne gave Dr. Micron her best winning smile. She almost looked innocent. Almost.

Micron fixed his eyes on George, then Jackbot, as he walked slowly toward them. "I see you've used

TinkerTech materials and tools to patch up this . . . this . . . What *is* it, exactly?"

"I'm Jackbot, Dr. Micron, sir," said Jackbot, holding out his right claw. "Very pleased to meet you."

"This is Jackbot," George said. "My personal robot and . . . friend."

"Friend?" said Dr. Micron.

"That's right," Jackbot piped up. "Ally. Companion. Bosom buddy."

Dr. Micron stared at Jackbot as if he were a puzzle he couldn't figure out. "He speaks very well, considering he's such a primitive design."

"Primitive?" said Jackbot. He backed away and placed an open pincer on his chest, as if he were insulted. "I can dance the Argentine tango and recite pi to twenty billion decimal places. I bet I could make a pretty mean soufflé as well. Can you do any of these things, Mr. Micron?"

"Jackbot . . ." George said under his breath to the robot. "Can it, would you please?"

"It's *Doctor* Micron, actually," said Dr. Micron, his face darkening.

"I know that," said Jackbot. "I was being deliberately rude."

Dr. Micron was silent for several long seconds. George watched him anxiously.

Suddenly Dr. Micron burst out laughing. He reached out and shook George's hand. "I have to hand it to you, young man. That's really something, what you've done there! The emotional simulations are . . . quite stupendous. And your name is?"

George exhaled in relief. "George Gearing, sir," he said, grinning.

Dr. Micron took in the name with a slight frown. "Gearing? Hmm. Are you related to the gentleman who runs the junkyard at the bottom of town?"

"That's my uncle Otto," said George.

"I see. Well, as you probably know, I'm Charles Micron. But call me Chip—all my friends do!" He winked.

"So—it's okay, then?" Anne asked.

"Well, let's put it this way—I won't tell anyone if you

don't! Now you'd better get out of here before someone else sees you."

He started to make his way back toward the door.

"It was an honor to meet you, sir!" George said.

"Ahem," said Jackbot, lifting his chin haughtily. "I still haven't forgotten that 'primitive' remark."

"Sorry, Jackbot," said Dr. Micron, turning briefly. As he left, he kept repeating, "Quite remarkable!"

The transport system whisked them back in no time. All the way, George kept thinking, *Dr. Micron . . .* the *Dr. Micron shook my hand!* All the way, Jackbot was muttering grumpily, "Primitive indeed! Who does he think he is?"

As soon as they left the chamber, the house said, "The time is nine thirty-four a.m. You are late for your math class, Miss Droid! Proceed to the classroom at once!"

George gulped. "I'm in big trouble," he said to Anne. "I'm so late for school! I have to go."

Anne's face fell a little. "No problem," she said. "Maybe—maybe I'll see you around?"

"Yeah, that would be good."

"I'll give you my number so you can put it in your smartphone—"

"I—I don't have a smartphone," George said, embarrassed. *Everyone* in Terabyte Heights had a smartphone.

"Okay, then, we'll do it the old-fashioned way!" said Anne. She took a pen and scribbled a number on the back of George's hand.

George grinned. "See you, then—and thanks for everything. Come on, Jackbot, we have minus thirty-four minutes to get to school!"

"Goodbye," the house said as George left.
"Please do not visit again during school hours. Recreational visits take place between six and eight p.m. on weekdays."

"Bye," said George, and started to sprint down the hill. He might just get to school by the end of first period.

Jackbot kept pace easily, his new hydraulic legs bouncing across the ground. "I know a shortcut."

"You do?" panted George. "How?"

"I can link with several GPS satellites, and I have a map of Terabyte Heights installed on my positronic memory drive!" Jackbot said. He veered off to the left and jumped over a wall.

George scrambled after him, already out of breath.

Jackbot led George down an alley, through a park where gardener-bots were watering the flowers, up some steps, and through a maze of side streets until finally they were standing opposite the steel-and-glass structure of Terabyte Heights Middle School. The front gates were closed and two robot cameras were mounted on top, swiveling as they surveyed the area, red eyes blinking.

"Wait!" George whispered. "They'll spot us and automatically report us to Principal Qwerty. Let's go around to the other entrance."

As George jogged down the service road that ran alongside the school, he saw Mr. Cog, the white-haired janitor, wheeling out a trash can.

"Hey, Mr. Cog!" George said. "We're running a bit late today—could you sneak us in?"

"Sure thing, George," said the janitor. He selected a key from the big bunch dangling from his belt. The keys were so heavy that they pulled his pants down low on that side, and he was always hitching them up. He inserted a key into the iron gate and let George and Jackbot in. "Last favor I'll be able to do you, though," he said. "They laid me off."

"What?" said George, shocked. "Why?"

Mr. Cog shrugged. "The principal said it was nothing personal. She just told me they were 'updating the system,' or something like that."

"But you've been here forever—it's not fair!"

Mr. Cog hitched his pants up. "Life ain't fair, my friend. I'll just have to find another job, is all."

"Who's going to be the new janitor, then?"

Mr. Cog shrugged again. "They didn't tell me nothing about that."

"Well—good luck, Mr. Cog," said George.

Mr. Cog smiled sadly and waved goodbye.

George and Jackbot walked quickly along a corridor and came out into the main hall just as the bell rang for the end of first period. Doors opened and students spilled out into the hall. Most had their own personal robots with them—tall, gleaming creations, some on wheels, some on legs, some with flashing displays on their chest panels. George was the only student with a homemade robot made out of spare parts.

At that moment, Patricia Volt appeared with her friends, carrying frappuccinos from Java, the coffee shop down the street where the cool kids all hung out. Patricia was the richest kid in school; she changed robots like she changed outfits. Her latest was a slender tennis robot named Bjorn, dressed all in white, sporting blond nylon hair and a headband.

Bjorn had a tennis-racket attachment on one arm and held Patricia's backpack in the other. Patricia looked up from the Series 6 SmartTablet in her hand and saw George hurrying by.

"Hey, Gearing!" she said. "Are you still dragging that sorry excuse for a robot around with you?"

Her friends sniggered.

"Leave Jackbot alone, Patricia," George said. "He's worth ten of your robots, anyway."

"Bjorn is worth eight and a half million dollars, so

I doubt that," Patricia sneered. "What do *you* think of
this pitiful little robot, Bjorn?"

Bjorn looked down at Jackbot. George realized that despite his fine new brain, Jackbot was still pretty scruffy. Even before being hit by a car, he'd looked secondhand, but now his body was badly scratched and dented.

"This is a substandard robot," Bjorn said. "This robot should be put out with the garbage immediately!"

The group laughed.

"So you play tennis?" Jackbot asked Bjorn.

"I am programmed to play at the international level," Bjorn said. "I serve at speeds of up to one hundred forty miles per hour. I can play two opponents simultaneously, with a win rate of ninety-eight percent."

"A simple yes would have been enough," said Jackbot. "Hey, Bjorn, I've been having a bit of trouble with my backhand. I wonder if you could give me some tips." He pulled a tennis ball from Bjorn's pocket. "Suppose someone serves to you at a velocity of one hundred thirty miles an hour, at an angle of thirty degrees, and I'm standing eight-point-seven feet back from the baseline—have you got all that?"

Bjorn's eyes started revolving. "Processing," he said.

"Okay, so how would you return this?" Jackbot threw the tennis ball at Bjorn. Automatically, Bjorn swung at it. He connected perfectly and the ball bounced off the wall, hit the ground, then smacked Patricia's cup right out of her hand. The coffee splashed all over her smart tablet, which fizzed, sparked, and went dead.

George gaped at Jackbot.

Patricia squealed. "You and that stupid robot!" she shouted at George. "Your uncle will be getting the bill for this!"

"But it wasn't Jackbot," George said. "Bjorn did it."

"Thanks for the help," Jackbot said to Bjorn. "Game, set, and match, I think."

All the students who'd been watching burst out laughing.

"I'll get you for this," Patricia said in a low voice. "You and that heap of junk of yours. That's a promise!"

She turned and flounced away, her followers scrambling to catch up.

George stood where he was, flabbergasted. "Jackbot— how did you do that?" he asked.

"A simple calculation," Jackbot said. "The angle of incidence equals the angle of deflection."

"But *why* did you do it?" George asked.

"They needed to be taught a lesson," Jackbot said.

George looked deep into Jackbot's glowing green eyes. "Let me get this straight," he said. "You can actually think for yourself?"

"Of course," said Jackbot. "You think I'm some sort of moron, idiot, or nincompoop?"

"No, I just—" George looked around to make sure no one was watching, and lowered his voice. "Look, is there really a *you* saying that? Or are you just a machine following a program?"

"I could ask you the same question!" Jackbot said.

George rubbed his temples. His mind was racing with the significance of what was happening. Two words floated to the surface, no matter how hard he tried to push them back. *Artificial Intelligence. AI, in its purest form.* It was the Holy Grail of robotics: a system that wasn't just preprogrammed responses, but tech that thought for itself. Not only did it think, but it felt emotions, had opinions, and had—dare he say it—a sense of humor. Could it be that the brain he'd cobbled together had produced something completely new?

George's train of thought was interrupted by a low humming noise. A gigantic robot was rolling along the hallway toward him. Its big square head almost brushed the ceiling. It had a rectangular mouth with large iron teeth, and slitlike golden eyes. Some sort of rodlike weapon extended from its left arm. Instinctively, George backed away.

But the robot ignored him. It eased to a halt in front of the puddle of spilled coffee, and the rod sprouted a mop head. The robot began to clean up the puddle. Then it picked up the coffee cup and popped it into a garbage hole in its middle. As the hole closed up, the robot played a little tune.

"What *is* that?" George wondered aloud.

"Tchaikovsky," said Jackbot. "*The Nutcracker Suite.*"

"Not the music—the robot!"

Just then, Principal Qwerty came around the corner with one of her students. Despite being only five feet tall, the principal had a fearsome reputation. Some kids said her hearing was genetically engineered to pick up the softest of students' whispers, even through solid walls. She missed *nothing.* "Oh, Caretaker!" she said. "Owen has forgotten the combination to his locker again. Could you open it for him with the master key?"

"Owen Hoffman, seventh grade, locker number four-two-seven," the Caretaker said. The mop head vanished and was replaced with a daggerlike metal attachment. The Caretaker rolled over to the locker and slid the spike into the lock. There was a brief whir, then the locker opened.

After Owen had retrieved his books, the teacher turned to George. "You'd better head to class, young man."

"So that's what took Mr. Cog's job!" George muttered.

"The Caretaker is much more efficient than the former janitor!" said Principal Qwerty. *She really* does *hear everything,* George thought. "It's TinkerTech's latest model, the first in Dr. Micron's new line. We are lucky to be beta testing it before it is mass-produced."

"But it's not fair for Mr. Cog to lose his job," George protested. "What if TinkerTech creates a robot to do *your* job?"

"Don't get smart with me," said the principal. "We have to move with the times. The Caretaker is at the cutting edge of educational security technology. With its key attachment, it can open any door in existence. Its sensors alert it to any cleaning job that needs doing throughout the building, and it responds immediately. And it doubles as the most reliable security guard you could wish for — it's programmed to arrest any intruder, and its eyes record every infraction into a data file. It never needs rest or sick days. Oh, and one more thing — it is excellent at enforcing school rules!" She turned to the intimidating robot. "Make sure this boy gets to class, won't you, Caretaker?"

"Affirmative," said the robot.

Principal Qwerty nodded crisply and walked away

with Owen. The Caretaker rolled toward George and Jackbot, towering over them. "George Gearing, sixth grade. Proceed to Ms. Hertz's IT class within ten seconds or punishment will result."

"What do you mean?" George said. "What kind of punishment?"

"Ten," said the Caretaker. "Nine. Eight. Seven . . ."

"Big deal, so you can count backwards!" said Jackbot. "So can a microwave."

George laughed.

The Caretaker's eyes flashed. "Insubordination detected! Commence punishment!"

It raised its arm and rotated its hand. An attachment like a crab's claw clicked out. The Caretaker rolled closer to George and reached toward the side of his head. "Earpinch initiated!"

George ducked and ran in the opposite direction, with Jackbot on his heels.

The Caretaker's shadow pursued them. "It's gaining on us!" said Jackbot.

They reached the stairs just ahead of the giant robot.

In three steps Jackbot reached the top. George raced after him.

The sound of the wheels stopped. On the second-floor landing, George turned and looked down. The Caretaker was standing in front of the stairs, bumping repeatedly against the bottom step.

"It can't get up the stairs!" George said.

"You need legs, Caretaker, that's what you need!" Jackbot said. To rub it in, he tap-danced.

The Caretaker watched them unblinkingly. "Your insolence is being digitally recorded," it said. Then it turned and rolled away.

George looked at Jackbot. "I didn't give you a stairs program, did I?"

Jackbot waved a pincer dismissively. "Who needs a program? It's not rocket science."

"Hey, it's good to be back!" Jackbot said as George opened the front door to his house after school. "What do you want to do, George? Chess? Basketball? Shall I perform *Swan Lake* for you?"

George laughed. "That sounds great, but I have homework to do."

"No, you don't," said Jackbot.

"*Really*, I do," said George. "A history essay on the rise and fall of Silicon Valley."

"*Really*, you don't," said Jackbot. He reached inside George's bag and pulled out his school tablet. "See? I did it for you." The screen scrolled through text.

George scanned the writing. "What? When did you do this? We've been together all day!"

"Not exactly," said Jackbot. "You were in the bathroom for four and a half minutes. I downloaded the most authoritative texts on the subject before putting together the essay."

"You did all that in less than five minutes?"

"I did that in one minute and forty-five seconds," said Jackbot. He closed the tablet. "I twiddled my thumbs for the other two minutes and forty-five seconds. Figuratively, of course."

"Jackbot, that's really nice of you, but . . . well, the teacher's bound to know I didn't write it."

"*Au contraire*," said Jackbot. "I took the liberty of assimilating all your written work from the past six months in order to replicate both your verbal patterns and most common typographical errors."

"But it's *wrong*," said George.

Jackbot's head slumped. "I'm sorry, George. I just wanted to help. I'll delete it, then." He opened the tablet.

"Wait! No!" said George. "There's no need for *that*. Just maybe don't do it again."

Jackbot's head perked up. "Okay, then. Basketball?"

"Let's go!" said George.

In the backyard, Jackbot stood opposite George, who had the ball. "Something tells me you're going to be good," said George, tossing the ball to his robot.

Jackbot spun the ball on his claw. "Let's see," he muttered. With a thrust of his arm he sent the ball flying up over the basket and onto the roof of the house.

"Bit too much power there," said George.

A couple of seconds later the ball bounced down the roof, hit the top of the wall, and spun back into the net.

"Three points," said Jackbot.

For the next half hour, George and Jackbot played. It was very different from their old games, when Jackbot had settled for standing on the sidelines and watching George miss.

Now George sensed that Jackbot was lowering his game so that they were evenly matched. The robot encouraged and coached him as they went. When George wanted to try a slam dunk, Jackbot had him climb on top of him to give him a boost.

"Are you sure I'm not going to crush you?" George asked.

"I'm stronger than I look," Jackbot replied. "Get on!"

George awkwardly climbed on top of Jackbot and aimed a jump at the hoop. He took a leap—and made it. The ball swished through the net as George hung triumphantly from the rim.

"He shoots—he scores!" Jackbot cheered.

A little while later, after a game of one-on-one, Jackbot was trying to teach George some other tricks.

"Try an overhead," said Jackbot.

George stood ten feet from the basket and checked over his shoulder. "Here goes!" he said.

He tossed the ball backwards.

There was a clatter, followed by a loud *CRACK!*

"What the—!" bellowed a voice.

In a flash, George remembered that the kitchen window had been open. *Oh, no,* he thought, his heart sinking. He turned slowly and saw his uncle Otto at the back door, a bagged lunch in his hand. Otto's carburetor lay in pieces on the ground at his feet, along with the bouncing basketball.

"Oops!" said Jackbot.

"You idiot!" Otto seethed. "I was fixing this up for a customer, and now it's more broken than when he gave it to me! That's a hundred dollars you've cost me right there!"

"I'm really sorry, Uncle Otto, honest," George said. "It was an accident."

"An *accident?*" Otto whispered, his voice dangerously low.

"Exactly," Jackbot piped up. "An unintended consequence." George silenced him with a look.

Otto's eyes bulged, and George half expected steam to jet out of his ears.

"You know what your problem is?" Otto said. "Your problem is that you don't know what's important in life. You never concentrate on what you ought to be doing, like fixing the house-bots. That's how accidents happen. From *not thinking.*" Otto shook his head. "You're just like your father."

George lowered his eyes.

"I don't want to speak ill of the dead," continued Otto, "but if your dad had thought about what he was doing the day of that accident instead of having *his* head up in the clouds, maybe he'd still be here. And then I wouldn't have to be looking after you all on my own. I'm only telling you this for your own good, George. Your *own good.*"

"Sorry," George muttered, staring at his shoes.

"Now, take that heap of junk"—Otto pointed at Jack-bot—"up to your bedroom and do your homework!"

Otto stalked back into the house.

Jackbot followed George up to his room. "Boy, what a grouch!" he muttered.

George shrugged. "That's just the way he is. He's . . . not a happy person." *I guess now I know it's because of me,* George thought.

"Maybe I could cheer him up?" Jackbot suggested. "Sing him a song? Tell a few jokes?"

"Uh, no, I have a feeling that might annoy him,"

George said. He sat on the bed and took out his blue marble. He rolled it between his fingers, comforted by the smooth feel of it.

"Hey, what's that, George?"

"Something my dad gave me when I was little," George said.

Jackbot patted George's shoulder with his claw. "Listen, it might be none of my business, but what happened to your mom and dad?"

George gripped the marble hard. He'd never really spoken to anyone about his parents; the fact that he had told Anne after just meeting her was totally out of character for him. And here he was talking about it again, twice in one day.

He took a deep breath. "I don't know much about it. They were in a car accident. The brakes went out on a mountain road outside of Terabyte Heights. Uncle Otto said my dad never took the Smart Car in for tune-ups when he should have."

"Accidents happen, George," said Jackbot. "They're no one's fault."

"I know that," said George. "Uncle Otto was upset. Mom was his sister."

He held the marble so tight his knuckles were white.

"Let's keep busy," said Jackbot breezily. "How about we look at these robots that need fixing?"

They spent the afternoon methodically repairing every single one of the house-bots. George lost himself in the work, and with Jackbot's help, they managed to identify and patch up most of the glitches. Even though George had thought fixing the robots would be impossible without a bunch of new parts, he was able to find ways to improve them using only what he had on hand. It was as if the act of reengineering Jackbot had opened up a new world in George's mind, where anything was possible.

By late evening, when Otto returned from the junk-yard, the house was spotless, and Mr. Egg was just placing a savory-smelling dish of meatloaf on the table.

Otto looked at it cautiously. George knew from experience that Mr. Egg's meatloaf was a thing to dread—but he had a feeling this time would be different.

"Don't be shy, give it a try!" sang Jackbot.

Otto took a cautious nibble and swallowed slowly. His watery eyes came to rest on George. "Not bad," he admitted. "Not bad at all." He wasn't exactly smiling, but as George watched his uncle eat every bite of meatloaf on his plate, he felt something very close to victory.

The next morning, the sun peeped in through George's bedroom window. George opened his eyes and yawned. His heart sank like a stone in a lake as he thought of the school day that stretched before him —

Wait! No! No, it didn't! Today was Saturday!

George had a day of freedom ahead of him. Uncle Otto would be at the junkyard, and George would be able to sleep in.

He closed his eyes, letting warm, shapeless thoughts drift over him.

DING-DONG!

The mists of sleep rolled away. George opened his eyes again.

DING-DONG!

Someone was ringing the doorbell. Repeatedly.

DING-DONG!

"Okay, okay," George mumbled. He rolled out of bed and shuffled downstairs in his pajamas. He opened the door to a familiar figure.

"Morning, Mrs. Glitch," George said. "I should be able to get to Lenny after breakfast—"

"No, it's not Lenny—it's HP, my home security robot."

George sighed. The retired line of Hector Protector robots was nothing but trouble. George had had to reprogram four of the robots on his block alone so that they wouldn't alert the police every time a fly landed on a window or a salesman knocked at a door. "What's wrong with it now?" he asked.

"It thinks *I'm* an intruder!" Mrs. Glitch said. "I went out to buy some milk and now it won't let me back in the house!"

"Sounds like its recognition circuits got scrambled," George said. "Either that or you've offended it somehow."

"Really? Do you think—?"

"No, I'm joking," said George. "Let me go get Jackbot. He'll sort this out quicker than I can."

Mrs. Glitch smiled. "So glad to hear your little friend is back on his feet. I knew you could fix him!"

George smiled and called into the house: "Hey, Jackbot!"

No reply.

"Jackbot?" he shouted.

Still nothing.

Strange. Where could he be?

"Hold on a minute, Mrs. Glitch," said George.

He searched the kitchen. The gardener-bot was watering the plants. Scrubby was hard at work on last night's meatloaf pan. Mr. Egg rolled forward and asked George if he'd prefer eggs Benedict or French toast.

But there was no Jackbot.

George started to feel worried. Could Jackbot be in the bathroom? No, he wasn't *that* human.

George ran upstairs and flung open every door. "Jackbot, quit playing around!"

The house was empty. George felt a sickening sensation build in his stomach.

"Any sign?" called Mrs. Glitch from the front door.

George returned to her, shaking his head.

Jackbot was missing.

Disappeared.

Vanished.

Gone.

5

For an hour, George combed every inch of the house for Jackbot. He looked in every room over and over again. He opened cupboards and closets and drawers, searched under beds and chairs and tables. He even called his uncle at the junkyard. But Uncle Otto didn't know where Jackbot was either.

George went out into the front yard, feeling desperate.

The old Jackbot would never have left home, but this new version—he was unpredictable.

"Hey, George!"

George looked up from a flower bed he was searching to see Anne standing at the end of the driveway. Beside her, Sparky stood wagging his metal tail. "Hi," George said, managing a tight smile.

Anne walked up to him. "I was just passing by," she said, "taking Sparky for a walk."

George raised an eyebrow. "You took a robotic dog across the entire town for a walk?"

Anne blushed. "I guess I was wondering how you and Jackbot were doing . . ." she said.

George swallowed hard. "Jackbot's gone," he said.

"Gone? What do you mean, gone?"

"I don't know! I woke up this morning and—and he's just vanished."

"Do you think he might still be damaged, after the accident? Maybe some wires got crossed and he wandered off?"

"I don't know," George said again. "He was working fine yesterday."

"You never know with robots," Anne said. "A loose connection somewhere inside, and suddenly they go haywire."

"I guess," said George. He'd seen enough of Mrs. Glitch's problem bots to know *that* was the truth. But somehow it just didn't feel right. "If he's wandered off, he'll have left some clues behind," he said. "I was just looking for him when you stopped by."

"We'll help you look!" Anne said. "Right, Sparky?"

Sparky barked and lowered his snout to the ground.

"He's programmed to identify close to two thousand individual smells," said Anne. "Have you got anything with Jackbot's scent on it?"

"Follow me," said George.

He led Anne and Sparky through the house. Normally, George would have felt embarrassed about where he lived. Compared with the Droid mansion, his house was like a shoebox. But at that moment all he could think about was Jackbot.

He found the basketball they'd been playing with the day before, and let Sparky smell it.

Sure enough, after a few seconds sniffing around outdoors, Sparky began to bark. He darted toward the bushes at the back of Uncle Otto's property. At the edge of the yard, on the concrete patio, George froze. A patch of bushes was damaged, the twigs bent and snapped. "Look!" he said, pointing near his feet at a black skid mark.

Anne frowned. "You think he came this way?"

"I think he was dragged," said George. "That looks like rubber from his treads."

"Why would anyone do that?" Anne asked.

"Oh, no," George murmured. "He's been kidnapped!"

Anne laughed. "Come on, George! Jackbot's kind of cute, but—well, no offense, but he can't be worth kidnapping! This is Terabyte Heights, remember? The town is full of state-of-the art robots worth millions of dollars. And Jackbot is . . . well . . ."

"He's the smartest robot I ever met!" said George.

"But George, everybody thinks their robot's smart! I even think Sparky's smart, although deep down I know he's dumb as a bag of hammers—"

George ignored her, his mind turning over. "Of course!" he said. "Patricia Volt!"

"Patricia Volt?" Anne said. "Her mom runs the Quality Control Department at TinkerTech, and her dad's the head of marketing. What's she got to do with this?"

George explained how Jackbot had totaled Patricia's tablet yesterday. "And she said she'd get back at me for it. This is her revenge!"

Anne nodded thoughtfully. "Sounds possible. Let's go ask her. I know where she lives—near us, in Binary Bluffs. I'll call the car."

Great, George thought as they waited. *Anne's house didn't like me—imagine what* Patricia's *will think!*

The Volt residence was not quite as impressive as Anne's house, but it was close. It was a big white building with turrets and a tower—like a castle, but more sleek and modern. The silver car stopped at the bottom of the driveway and encouraged them not to be too long, because it was due for a tune-up at ten o'clock.

George knocked on Patricia's door and it replied, "Welcome, stranger. Your request for entry has been logged and brought to the attention of the residents. Please wait patiently."

The screen beside the door lit up with Patricia's face. The girlish pigtails and bow in her hair were completely at odds with the vicious scowl on her face.

"What are *you* doing in Binary Bluffs?" she said, squinting at George. Then she noticed Anne and did a double take. "And what are *you* doing with *him?*"

"Never mind about that," George blurted out. "Just give me back my robot!"

Patricia put on a tremendous performance of appearing astonished. Her exquisitely sculpted eyebrows disappeared into her tousled bangs and her mouth formed an O of surprise. "You have . . . a *robot?*" she said.

"Cut the act, Trish," said Anne. "Jackbot. Have you seen him?"

"Oh, *that* thing? I'm sorry, I didn't realize. I thought it was just a pile of scrap metal that this loser carts around with him."

George was so angry, he thought he was going to explode. But before he could say anything, Anne took a step forward.

"Seriously, Trish," she said in a soft voice that was almost menacing. "Jackbot has gone missing. I'd hate to have to bring my father into this."

Patricia looked spooked. "Okay, okay. Just wait a minute." The screen clicked off. George could imagine her calculating and then deciding that she couldn't be rude to Anne, daughter of the famous and powerful Professor Droid. A few seconds later, the door swung open and Patricia stood there in the flesh. Bjorn hovered behind her.

"For the record, I have no idea where that little robot is," Patricia said. "If he's lost, that's too bad, but it's got nothing to do with me."

"Yesterday you said you were going to get back at me for what Jackbot did," said George. "And today, Jackbot's gone missing. Don't you think that's a little bit of a coincidence?"

"Yes, I do," said Patricia. "I think it's a total coincidence!"

George was figuring out what to say next when he heard a rumbling sound grow louder behind him.

He turned to see one of the city's huge robotic garbage trucks coming up the road. Nothing unusual there. He turned back to Patricia, wondering if he should try to force his way into the house.

She was looking over his shoulder. "That's weird," she muttered. "It's not garbage day . . ."

The truck revved its engines ferociously, and George saw Patricia's eyes go wide.

"Um . . ." said Anne.

George heard a loud bang and turned to see the Volts' mailbox spinning through the air as the truck mounted the sidewalk and careened up the driveway. Anne's car said something about a "collision hazard" two seconds before the truck flattened it like a tin can. "Sparky!" Anne shouted in panic. Broken glass and metal exploded beneath the truck's caterpillar tracks. It pressed on, heading straight toward them. Its headlights looked like two

eyes filled with malice, and its powerful crusher opened and closed like a set of jaws.

"It must be malfunctioning!" said George.

"Stop it!" yelled Patricia. "Bjorn, do something!"

In a split second, Bjorn ejected a stream of tennis balls from his stomach compartment. They bounced off the truck's grill harmlessly.

"I think it's going to take more than a strong serve to stop it," said George. A claw scooper extended from the back of the truck and waved like a scorpion's tail.

George backed into the house and pulled Anne along with him. She was pale, still staring at the remains of her dad's car. "Oh, I'm grounded," she groaned. "Definitely grounded."

"Come on!" George shouted.

Patricia slammed the door closed. "Let's just wait for it to go past," said Patricia. "Someone call TinkerTech. They'll know what to—"

CRUNCH.

The metal scoop tore through the front door like it was tissue paper.

George wasn't sure who screamed the loudest.

"Run!" he shouted.

"Bjorn, cover us!" said Patricia.

The three of them turned and fled toward the back of the house. George looked over his shoulder and saw Bjorn standing bravely in front of the metal jaws. "He doesn't stand a chance against that thing!" George said.

Two pincers reached out from the truck's flanks and dragged the tennis-bot into its jaws. Bjorn vanished with a metal screech, shouting "Deuuuuuce!"

"We can't run!" said George. "It's too fast!"

"You have a better idea?" said Patricia.

"Keep it distracted," said George. He peeled away from Patricia and Anne and headed up the stairs. The truck finished chewing Bjorn and its camera swiveled, as if it was searching for something. It lumbered closer and closer to Patricia and Anne.

George waited until the truck was level, then threw himself off the stairs and into its cab. He stamped on the brake and twisted the steering wheel.

The truck didn't stop, but now it seemed to be

confused. Through the windshield, George could see its camera swiveling in circles, and it was waving its giant pincers around wildly. Patricia shrieked as the sharp metal claws came within inches of her face, but Anne picked up an iron poker from the fireplace and walloped the claws aside. "I got plenty more where that came from!" she yelled.

George saw a glass panel marked M.O.

Manual override. Of course!

He raised his foot and kicked the panel with all his might. The glass shattered, and on the other side was a lever.

The truck was still going forward. A few more feet and it would crush Anne and Patricia against an inside wall of the house. "George!" Anne screamed. "I can't hold this thing off any longer!"

George yanked the lever.

The truck bucked, hurled him against the dashboard, and stopped.

George breathed a sigh of relief and peered through the cab.

Patricia lowered her hands from her face and looked around, aghast. Pieces of plaster and masonry had collapsed from the ruined walls. Dust was everywhere.

"Is everyone okay?" George called out.

"Get that thing out of my house—now!" Patricia said. "It almost killed us!"

"Hold on a minute!" said George. He scanned the controls, saw a switch labeled REVERSE, and pressed it.

The truck didn't move, but its rear container began to rise up and over the cab. It hovered over Patricia and the rest of her living room.

"Oh, no . . ." said George.

The container tipped, and a wave of garbage spilled out of it—mostly right on top of Patricia. George saw fish heads, rotting fruits and vegetables, bones, cans, bottles, soup, coffee grounds, jelly, dirty diapers, and other things too disgusting to describe in the multicolored avalanche. The deluge didn't let up for a good ten seconds, after which Patricia stood covered from head to toe in an unspeakable mess.

"Sorry," George squeaked, "wrong button." He tried a

couple of others, and finally the truck backed slowly out of the house. Shakily, George climbed down from the cab and walked inside again, just as he heard the scampering of paws. Sparky ran up to Anne as she climbed out of the dusty mess toward him.

"You're alive!" she said. She beamed at George. "He must have escaped from the car before the truck hit it!"

The stink from the garbage was overpowering. Patricia was still frozen on the spot, buried up to her chest. Her mouth was moving but hardly making a sound.

"Sorry . . . um, really sorry," said George.

Patricia finally detached herself from the garbage and pulled something moldy from her hair. Her glowering eyes settled on George.

Something told him she wasn't too happy.

6

George, Anne, and Patricia were just coming out of the house when a TinkerTech security car screeched to a halt in front of the Volt residence. Or what was left of it. As an officer climbed out of the car, he pulled off his mirrored shades and stared up at the house. The front door and porch were completely gone, chewed through by the marauding truck. Garbage was strewn everywhere.

The security officer strode up the front yard toward them, flanked by two seven-foot-tall silver robots. His badge read OFFICER DONGLE. According to their badges, the robots' names were XZ1P75-0 and XZ1P75-1.

"What is the meaning of this?" demanded the officer.

"We have a report that someone hijacked a TinkerTech truck and emptied its load."

"Yeah, he did!" Patricia said, pointing at George. The movement caused a whiff of stink to waft through the air. Officer Dongle wrinkled his nose and took a step backwards.

"Wait! Hold on!" said George. "I didn't hijack it! It was malfunctioning—I was trying to stop it from killing us!"

"It's true," Anne said. "George saved our lives!"

"Arrest him!" said Patricia.

"I intend to," said Officer Dongle. "Miss Droid, you should go home. Miss Volt, you should take a shower. And you"—he pointed at George—"you're coming with us. You can explain yourself at TinkerTech HQ."

"But I'm telling you the truth!" George said. "I only tampered with it after it went berserk."

"Liar!" said Patricia. "You seriously expect me to believe it was a coincidence that you arrived just before that thing? You're always tinkering with robots. You *made* it attack my house!"

"The truck's black box will show what really happened," said George.

"Yes, it will," said the officer. "XZ1P75-0, retrieve the recorder. XZ1P75-1, take that boy into custody!"

One robot shot over to the truck while the other made its way toward George. Anne jumped into its path. "Hey, no! You can't! This is a mistake."

The end of the robot's arm crackled with electric current. "Stand back, miss," the robot said.

"It's okay," said George to Anne. "I'll go—I'm sure this will get cleared up soon."

George walked to the security car, one robot beside him and the other not far behind.

George had passed the gleaming towers of TinkerTech HQ hundreds of times—it was the most recognizable building in Terabyte Heights—and he'd always dreamed about venturing inside. Yesterday that dream had come true when he'd visited the TinkerTech workshop, and today he was going through the front doors.

He just wished the circumstances were a little different.

Tall glass doors opened into a huge atrium, with palm trees soaring upward and brightly colored parrots flitting about. They must be robot parrots, George guessed. You wouldn't want real parrots pooping on people's heads.

A bespectacled receptionist robot nodded and smiled at them as Officer Dongle signed them in.

"I gotta go make my report," the officer said to the security robots. "Take the suspect up to Professor Droid's office."

George tried to keep his cool. Professor Droid *had* to believe his story, and the black box would back him up. He just wished Anne were there too. Or Jackbot.

The robots took George's arms and marched him toward the elevator. The doors swished open, then shut behind them. George saw that there were ninety floors.

"You don't have to hold me all the way," said George. "I'm not going anywhere."

The robots remained silent and didn't budge.

The elevator had glass sides, and as it rocketed skyward, George had an incredible view of the inner workings of TinkerTech Enterprises. He saw massive open-plan departments where robots were being put through their paces, practicing moves and actions, watched by white-coated men and women with clipboards. There were robots playing football, chess, and trumpets; robots riding motorbikes, cooking omelets, dealing cards.

The elevator came to a stop at the ninetieth floor.

"Have a nice day," said the elevator as the doors opened.

"I'll try," said George.

"Go to the door at the end of the hallway," said XZ1P75-0.

"Sit and wait for Professor Droid," said XZ1P75-1.

"Don't try to run away," said XZ1P75-0.

"Or we'll get you," said XZ1P75-1.

George set off down the long corridor. It was so thickly carpeted that his feet made no sound. The door at the end was about fifteen feet high and made of dark, polished wood. A gold plaque said PROFESSOR A. I. DROID, HEAD OF TINKERTECH.

George didn't know whether to knock. On the wall there was a picture of Professor Droid as a young man, standing beside one of his earliest creations: a robot designed to play tic-tac-toe.

"Sit," said a voice behind him.

George turned around and saw that a metal seat had extended from the wall. He sat down awkwardly. At the other end of the hallway, the security robots were still standing by the elevator, watching him silently.

George's heart was pounding. He licked his lips, wishing for a glass of water.

Then he felt something warm in his pants pocket. He looked down. A blue glow was shining through the material. He put his hand in and felt the familiar shape of his marble. He pulled it out.

"Huh?" he muttered to himself.

The marble was radiating a blue light. How was that even possible? He hadn't known there was a power source inside. The glass was clear, not cloudy like before. He could almost make out something . . .

He lifted the marble to his eye for a closer look, and realized the curved surface of the marble was acting like a magnifying glass. There was some sort of tiny LCD screen in there, and . . . *writing!* As he watched, the text on the screen started scrolling swiftly downward. The words were still too small and were scrolling too fast for George to read much of the information, but he did see the same two words over and over again: PROJECT MERCURY.

George felt a tingle over his skin. What did that mean? And why was his marble lighting up now?

The seat beneath him vanished back into the wall, and he fell to the floor.

"Stand," said a voice.

"Thanks for the warning," said George, climbing to his feet and pocketing the marble. He'd have to think about the marble later. The massive wooden door slowly began to open.

Professor Droid stood inside. George recognized the distinguished, silver-haired man he'd seen in the pictures at Anne's house. Only now, he wasn't smiling.

"George Gearing," Professor Droid said drily, "please come in."

George entered the office. To his surprise, it was quite old-fashioned, with a huge desk and leather chairs. The lights on the walls had old-fashioned switches, and the shelves were lined with books. Paper ones.

One side of the office consisted of floor-to-ceiling windows, through which George could see the whole of Terabyte Heights spread out beneath. The town planners had designed it to look like a circuit board from the air, and George couldn't help but grin in wonder.

"Something funny?" said Professor Droid.

"No, sir," said George.

The professor sat in a chair behind the desk and gestured toward another chair. "Sit down," he said.

George sat cautiously, half expecting the seat to move at the last moment or to send an electric shock through his body.

"Don't be scared," said Professor Droid. "It's just a chair."

He regarded George intently for a while without speaking. Then he said, "Hijacking TinkerTech property. Criminal damage to TinkerTech property. Criminal damage to the Volts' house. These are very serious offenses. Do you have anything to say?"

"I swear, I wasn't responsible," said George. "The black box will prove it's true."

Professor Droid steepled his fingers. "It's funny you should say that, because we recovered the vehicle's recorder and it's completely blank."

George felt the blood drain from his face. "Blank?"

"That's right," said Professor Droid. "Wiped clean."

"How can that be?" said George.

"Why don't you tell me?" said the professor. He stared down his long nose at George. "I'm actually quite curious to know."

"Wait . . . You don't think . . . You can't believe that *I* had something to do with it?" said George.

Professor Droid laid a hand on his desk, and a section of the wood slid back to reveal a screen. "Miss Volt, in her statement, says that you and she have been long-time enemies."

"Yeah, I can't stand her," said George, then quickly added, "but I wouldn't destroy her house!"

"She also said that you consider yourself a bit of a robotics engineer, and that you're jealous of her relative wealth."

"But—"

"Mr. Gearing," interrupted the professor, "right now, it isn't looking good for you."

"You have to believe me!" George said. "You can ask Anne—your daughter! She was there. She'll vouch for me!"

Professor Droid raised his gray eyebrows. "I love my

daughter dearly, of course. But I could not say she is the most reliable witness in the world. If you knew all of the misadventures she has gotten herself into in the past . . . But let's leave that aside. Do you deny that you climbed into the cabin of the TinkerTech garbage truck without authorization?"

"Well, no, but you see—"

"Do you deny," said Professor Droid, "that you activated the manual override?"

"I had to!"

"And do you deny that as a direct result, the entire load of garbage was emptied inside the Volts' house?"

"But that part was an accident . . ."

Professor Droid raised his hand. "Then there really is nothing more to discuss. You have confessed to three serious offenses. I am turning you over to the city police."

"Please," George said desperately. "I had no choice!"

Professor Droid swiped the screen, and a keypad came up.

George couldn't believe what was happening. The police! What would happen to him? Would he be sent to prison? Did they send ten-year-olds to prison? And what would Uncle Otto say? There was absolutely no way he'd believe George's version of the story. *You never think, George! You had this coming, George . . .*

Professor Droid had begun to stab at numbers on the keypad.

There was a soft tap at the door.

Professor Droid looked up, frowning. He clicked his fingers, and the door opened.

Dr. Micron entered the room. "Really sorry to interrupt, Professor Droid," he said. He spotted George and did a double take.

"Can't it wait, Chip?" said Professor Droid. "I just have to deal with this boy—"

"Gearing, isn't it?" said Dr. Micron.

"You know him?" said Professor Droid, surprised.

"Not exactly," said Dr. Micron, searching George's face. George wanted the chair to swallow him up. If Dr. Micron were to mention that George had snuck into the workshop from Professor Droid's home, that would be it! He did his best, with furtive shakes of his head, to let the man know this wasn't the time to say anything.

"Well, he's in a lot of trouble," said Professor Droid. "I'm about to have the police take him away."

"You're kidding!" said Dr. Micron. "I'm a pretty good judge of character, and I'm sure that whatever he did was done with the best of intentions. He's not a criminal, Professor. I'd stake my reputation on it."

George's heart lifted, and he glanced at Professor Droid.

"He's caused thousands of dollars' worth of damage to TinkerTech and private property," said Professor Droid.

"Is this true?" Dr. Micron asked George.

"No!" said George. "I mean, it happened, but it wasn't my fault. I was just trying to help."

"The boy seems honest to me, Professor," said Dr. Micron. "Why not give him a break this time?"

Professor Droid's mouth formed a hard line, but finally he nodded. "Well, all right, then," he said slowly.

"I'll trust your judgment on this one, Chip." He turned and stared at George. "Looks like it's your lucky day. You can go. Just think twice before you tamper with TinkerTech property again!"

George decided it wasn't worth protesting anymore. "Of course," he said. "Thank you, sir."

"What was it you wanted to see me about, anyway?" asked the professor.

Dr. Micron waved a hand. "Don't worry, it's not urgent. I'll see George out, shall I?"

They took their leave and walked down the hall together. "Thank you so much!" said George as they reached the elevator. XZ1P75-0 and XZ1P75-1 parted to let them pass.

"You're welcome," said Dr. Micron. "I know you're not a bad kid. But tell me this—why *did* you climb into the truck?"

"It's a long story," said George.

"Try me," said Dr. Micron.

George was still telling his version of events long after the elevator reached the ground floor.

" . . . and it all started because I was looking for Jackbot!" said George.

"That's the robot I met in the workshop, right?" said Dr. Micron.

George nodded sadly. "He's missing."

"That's too bad."

"Anne thinks he just wandered off, but I'm sure he wouldn't do that. I think he's been taken."

Dr. Micron laughed. "Oh, I don't think that's likely. Didn't he have a tracker?"

George shook his head. "Until yesterday, he wasn't exactly what you'd call cutting-edge technology."

Dr. Micron escorted George to the front doors. "I'm sorry that you've lost your robot, George. Trust me, I know that robots aren't just programming and parts. They can be friends, too."

"Jackbot was my best friend," George said.

Dr. Micron patted him on the back. "Don't spend too much time worrying about him, kid," he said. "These things tend to find their way back on their own." He turned back to the building, then seemed to remember something and reached into his inside pocket. "Before you go, I'd like to give you a little gift. Something to keep you company until you get your friend back."

He took out a silver object the size of a bullet and placed it in George's hand. After a moment, it twitched, then unfurled.

It was a tiny robot, with a little goggle-eyed head and two antennae that glowed like fiber-optic cable. Its mothlike wings began to whir, and it rose in the air and hovered in front of George's face, cocking its head inquisitively.

"What is it?" said George.

"It's a pocket robot. A new line I've been working on. Perhaps you could test it out for a few days, then give us some feedback?"

George's eyes bugged. "A prototype?"

The robot moth settled on his shoulder. George could feel its feathery wings tickle his cheek.

"I think it likes you!" said Dr. Micron.

"It's fantastic!" George said.

"Take a TinkerTech car home," said Dr. Micron. "I'll authorize it."

"Wow—I don't know what to say," said George.

"Just don't override the controls!" said Dr. Micron with a wink.

As George opened the front door, his new
robot moth fluttered into the house at his side, flying
in effortless little loops. The house felt very quiet. *Uncle
Otto must still be at the junkyard,* George thought.

George went into the kitchen and asked Mr. Egg to
pour him a glass of orange juice. The robot not only did it,
but added a fresh orange slice and a little umbrella to the
glass as well. Normally George would have been ecstatic,
but the fancy drink only made him think of Jackbot.

George flopped on the sofa, and his spirits sagged
too. He might have narrowly escaped the police station,
but he wasn't any closer to finding his friend.

As he sipped his juice, he remembered the blue

marble and took it out from his pocket. The moth-bot hovered close by. But the marble was no longer lit up from inside. It had gone cloudy again. Had he imagined it—the screen, "Project Mercury," and all of the other writing? He held the marble up to the light, but it remained stubbornly opaque.

George heard the sound of his uncle's pickup truck scraping to a halt on the gravel outside. The engine died. A moment later George heard Otto's key in the door. George wondered about the best way to explain what had happened at Patricia's. Maybe he should just keep quiet about the whole thing.

One look at Otto's face was enough to tell him that his uncle already knew.

"Hi," said George. It came out in a squeak.

"I got a call from TinkerTech Enterprises when I was at the junkyard," Otto said, his voice eerily calm. "What do you think that was about, George? Do you have any idea?"

"Um, I guess it was about the thing with the garbage truck."

"Yes!" shouted Uncle Otto, all calm fleeing his face. "The thing with the garbage truck! Breaking my carburetor wasn't enough for you, was it? You wanted to try for something bigger, so you destroyed a TinkerTech truck!"

"But it's all taken care of, Uncle Otto. I promise!"

"We're darn lucky they're not making us pay for the damage—we'd be bankrupt and then some! You may have gotten away with it in the eyes of the authorities, but I'm not so forgiving, George. You're grounded. All summer. Any spare time, you're going to be helping me out at the junkyard. I could use another pair of hands."

"But Uncle Otto!" said George. "I've got to find Jackbot!"

"That heap of trash is probably rusting in a gutter somewhere," said Otto. "It's time you stopped messing around with robots and concentrated on your schoolwork."

The moth-bot chose that moment to zip across the room and loop around Otto's head.

"What the—!" he said, swinging his beefy arms and missing. "What is that thing? Get it away from me!"

"They gave it to me at TinkerTech. It's a pocket robot in the shape of a moth," George explained.

"Don't make me take a fly swatter to it," grunted Otto. "I'm gonna take a shower. Try to keep yourself out of trouble while I'm gone." He stomped upstairs, and a few minutes later, George heard the rush of water.

George held out his hand, and the moth-bot came and settled on his fingers. "It's so unfair!" he said to the bot. "How am I supposed to track down Jackbot if I can't even leave the house? Uncle Otto's going to watch me like a hawk!"

Suddenly George remembered Mrs. Glitch and her security robot. Had she been shut out of her house all day? He sprang up and rushed to the door, then remembered he was grounded.

He cocked his ear. Uncle Otto liked to spend a while in the shower. Then he'd have to trim his beard and get dressed. George thought he probably had twenty minutes. He slipped outside. The little moth fluttered after him.

"Oh, George!" said Mrs. Glitch as she opened her front door. "I'm so glad to see you!"

"You got back in the house, then?"

"Eventually," said Mrs. Glitch. "I had to get Lenny to sneak up behind HP and switch it off. But now I don't have any home security . . ."

"Let me take a quick look at it," George said. "I'll see what I can do."

Throwing curious glances at the robot moth, Mrs. Glitch led George into the back room, where HP was sitting motionless on the floor. It was a humanoid robot with a TV screen for a head. More than a little creepy, really—which is probably why the model had been retired.

George took out his screwdriver and opened the back of HP's head. "I see the problem," he said to Mrs. Glitch. "See where that wire's loose? That's what links the recognition circuit to the behavioral program. Easy peasy."

He pushed the wire back into place and tightened a screw on top of it. "It should be fine now."

George closed up HP's head and flicked the ON switch at the back of its neck.

HP slowly rose to its feet. Its TV-screen head swiveled to look at Mrs. Glitch and George. "Loretta Glitch. George Gearing," it said in a slow, monotonous voice. "Access authorized."

"Oh, thank you so much, George!" said Mrs. Glitch.

"Anytime. Now you can sleep easy knowing that HP's on the job again!" Suddenly, George felt a rush of adrenaline as an idea sprang into his mind. "Wait a minute! HP would have been watching the house last night, right?"

"Why, yes, it always stands guard outside the house at night."

"Would you mind if I checked the footage?" asked George.

"Not at all."

It might be nothing, George thought, *but it's worth a shot.*

"HP?" he said. "Could you run last night's security video, starting at nine p.m.?"

"Affirmative."

A picture appeared on HP's screen. It was dark, and

showed Mrs. Glitch's yard and the road in front of George's house. Clouds drifted across the moon, and a car or two sped by.

"Could you speed it up?" George said. "Increase by a factor of thirty-two."

The label "×32" appeared at the top corner of the screen. The clouds no longer drifted, but raced across the moon, and the moon itself could be seen inching higher in the sky. Then a dark blur rushed across the screen.

"Stop!" said George. "Run the last minute again. At normal speed."

The video reversed and played again. A huge shadow spread from the left side of the screen as something approached the Gearing yard. George saw a gigantic figure with a big square head rolling on wheels toward his house. The glowing eyes glanced for a moment into the camera.

George lurched back. "It's the Caretaker!"

"Who?" said Mrs. Glitch.

George watched the footage, speechless, as the

Caretaker rolled up to the front door of his house. In a matter of seconds it stooped under the doorframe and entered. *The master key attachment,* George thought. *It must have used that to break into the house!* George shook his head, dismayed, but it was all falling into place.

In less than a minute the Caretaker emerged again, carrying George's friend. The thief closed and locked the door. Suddenly Jackbot came to life and pushed his way out of the Caretaker's grip. The Caretaker didn't seem to have expected that, but it quickly recovered and chased Jackbot into the bushes off the back patio. There, it dragged Jackbot back out of the bushes and used one of its attachments to turn the battered bot off for good. *That must be where the skid marks came from,* thought George. After a moment, both robots vanished off the side of the screen.

But why? What would the Caretaker want with Jackbot? Well, the Caretaker didn't *want* anything. It was just a robot. It did what it was told. If it had kidnapped Jackbot, it was because someone had told it to.

The name that sprang to George's mind made no sense.

"Are you all right, George?" said Mrs. Glitch. "You've gone pale."

"Not really," said George. "I've got to go."

8

George made it back to his house with time to spare before his uncle finished getting dressed. His mind kept turning over the same question: *Why would Dr. Micron want to steal Jackbot?*

He checked the dim and blurred number on the back of his hand and picked up his old-fashioned phone to dial it.

Anne answered on the third ring.

"It's me," said George.

"Are you okay?" she said. "I called my dad but he said he was too busy to talk."

"It all got sorted out," said George. *By Dr. Micron—*

but why? "Listen, Anne. I think I know who stole Jackbot. It was Dr. Micron."

Anne laughed. "That's funny," she said. "Was he looking for parts?"

"I'm serious!" said George. "It was one of his robots that snuck into my house and kidnapped Jackbot."

"Slow down," said Anne. "You're jumping to conclusions again. Remember what happened with Patricia—"

Another thought tumbled into George's brain. "And what about the garbage truck? Maybe it wasn't a malfunction. What if it was trying to kill me?"

"George, you're freaking me out," said Anne. "Why in the world would Dr. Micron want Jackbot?"

It came to George like a flash of light. "Because of his AI," he said. "Of course! Dr. Micron saw that Jackbot's programming was revolutionary. He wants to copy it and take the credit."

Anne was silent for a moment. George heard her take a deep breath. "George, you've got to stop and think for a second. Next to my dad, Dr. Micron is the greatest robotics engineer in the world. Jackbot . . . he's quirky, but—"

"You don't get it," said George, his frustration mounting. "You don't know Jackbot like I do. It's not a quirk—he's really thinking for himself. It's like he's more than just a robot . . . he's his own person." George felt tired of trying to convince people he was telling the truth. "Look, you can believe me or not—but I'm going after Jackbot. Will you help me?"

"I'm not going to help you make a fool of yourself, no. I've already done that today," said Anne.

George heard a sound beside his ear and saw the moth-bot hovering close to his head.

"Fine," he said to Anne. "I'll do this on my own." He hung up the phone with a satisfying slam. *Let's see her do that with a smartphone,* he thought.

But after a moment, he stopped feeling satisfied and just felt alone. He turned to the moth. "Looks like it's just you and me, buddy," he said.

Suddenly, the moth-bot's little eyes turned bright red. A long, whippy steel tongue unfurled from its

mouth, and it made
a sudden stab at
George's hand.

"What? Hey!"
George jerked out
of the way as a clear
liquid dripped from the
moth-bot's tongue and landed
on the sofa with a hiss. The
fabric sizzled and turned
black.

Acid!

The robot was coming
at him again. Straight at
his face.

George ducked.

The creature whizzed over his head, close enough to
ruffle his hair.

"Hey, stop!" shouted George, backing away.

"What's goin' on down there?" Otto yelled from
upstairs.

George ran around the room, pursued by the moth-bot. Tiny jets of acid scorched the curtains, the carpet, the table. George ran into the kitchen. He tried to slam the door closed, but the robot zipped through the crack just in time. George seized a frying pan.

"What can I get you, George?" said Mr. Egg calmly. "An omelet? A frittata, perhaps?" Since being fixed, the cook-bot was much more civilized.

George swung at the moth-bot and hit it with a metallic *ping!*

The tiny bot flew across the kitchen, bounced off the wall, and fell into the sink's garbage disposal. George leaped forward and turned on the switch. With a terrible squeal, the metal blades spun and then ground to a halt. Smoke rose from the sink.

George peered inside the disposal, frying pan raised. The moth was a twisted mess, its eyes dim. Its acid-spitting days were over.

Sweat prickled on George's forehead as he sat down at the table.

Uncle Otto burst into the room, a towel wrapped

around his waist. "Would you please stop that racket?" he said. "What does a guy have to do for some peace and quiet?" His nose twitched as he picked up the scent of charred machinery, and he strode over to George. "What did you do to the sink?"

George was too lost in thought to respond.

The moth-bot had just tried to kill him! Of course it had. It was a gift from Dr. Micron, after all. He must have overheard George's conversation with Anne.

"Steak sandwich, Otto?" said Mr. Egg.

"No, shut up!" said Otto. "George, answer me!"

And if Dr. Micron heard me speaking to Anne . . .

George stood up quickly. "I've got to go," he said. "Anne's in danger."

"You're not going anywhere!" said Otto.

George ran past him and out the front door.

"Come back here right now, young man!" bellowed his uncle.

George didn't stop running until he reached Anne's house in Binary Bluffs. He hammered on the door, then bent over double on her doorstep, dripping with sweat and gasping for breath.

"Go away," said the house. "No unauthorized visitors are welcome at this time."

"Anne!" shouted George. "Open the door!"

"The door will not open," said the house. "You are not permitted to enter. No unauthorized visitors are welcome at this time."

George banged on the door again. He heard Sparky barking inside.

"Is that you, George?" said Anne's voice from the other side of the door. "Have you lost your mind?"

"Thank goodness you're all right!" said George. "Let me in, quick!"

George heard Anne trying to turn the door handle.

"I can't open it," said Anne. "House! Let me out!"

"No unauthorized visitors are welcome at this time," said the house.

"Anne, this is serious!" said George. "You're in danger! You have to get that door open."

"What?" said Anne. "George, if this is more nonsense about Dr. Micron . . ."

"He just tried to kill me!" said George.

The door handle rattled again.

"Open this door, house," said Anne. *"Now!"*

"The door will not open. You are not permitted to leave," said the house. "No unauthorized exits at this time."

"Fine," said Anne. "You asked for it!"

"What are you doing?" called George.

"Wait and see!" said Anne. "Stand back!" George heard her footsteps retreating, with Sparky barking and pattering along beside her.

"Hey, get away from that!" said the house.

George took a few steps back from the door and shifted his weight from foot to foot, wishing he knew what was going on. He scanned the street outside, just in case there were any more rogue garbage trucks around.

A loud *BOOM!* sounded from inside the house, and the door shook.

The house groaned.

"Grrooooghellllaghblmf," it said. "No unauthorized bleeeerkh. *Gahhhhh.*"

The lock clicked and the door swung open.

George stepped into the house.

Anne and Sparky appeared at the end of the hallway. Anne was grinning, and Sparky's tongue was lolling out as if he was pleased with himself as well. A cloud of smoke was drifting up behind them. The maid-bot in the white apron, which was cleaning the paintings on the walls, continued dusting as if nothing had happened.

"What did you do?" said George.

"I got Sparky to chew through the wires of the central controls."

"Nice one," said George. "Now do you believe me?"

"What, just because my house is being stubborn?"

"Don't you see?" said George. "Dr. Micron's taken control!"

"I don't believe in conspiracy theories," said Anne. "But come in, anyway."

As George walked toward Anne, the maid-bot rolled toward the middle of the hallway. It pointed its feather duster. The feathers fell off to reveal a bunch of glinting metal spikes beneath.

"Targets detected," it said in a soft voice with a slight

French accent. "Proceed to eliminate targets. Method selected: stabbing with sharp things."

"Um, excuse me?" said Anne.

As the maid-bot advanced toward them, Sparky barked at it.

George grabbed Anne and tugged her toward another door. "Quick!" he said.

The door behind them opened, and out came a state-of-the-art chef-bot wearing a tall white hat. It was carrying a meat cleaver.

"Targets detected," it said. "Proceed to eliminate targets. Method selected: spatchcock."

George had no clue what that meant, but he didn't like the sound of it. He looked at Anne. "Now what?"

"Through the dining room!" Anne said. "It leads out to the backyard."

She ran to a side door but before she got there, it opened and a green gardener-bot came in from the yard, sporting a coiled rubber hose and a sprinkler on its head. It was opening and shutting a pair of shears. "Targets detected," it said. "Proceed to eliminate targets. Method selected: pruning."

A handyman robot, dressed in white, appeared

through another side door. It was carrying a spinning electric drill. It said something. George couldn't hear the words above the loud, ugly whine of the drill, but he was pretty sure he got the gist.

He turned to Anne. "How does that conspiracy theory sound now?"

9

The killer robots were getting closer.

Sparky didn't know which way to turn, and ran around planting himself in front of the various attackers. The chef-bot looked down at him for a moment, then kicked him.

CLANG! Sparky went tumbling head over heels, yelping. He got to his feet with difficulty—one of his legs was broken.

"Sparky!" said Anne.

"Anne," said George, "we have to get out of here!"

"Upstairs!" Anne said. She ducked under the chopping shears of the gardener-bot, scooped Sparky off the floor, and ran up the broad, curving staircase. Halfway to the top she stopped to look back.

George dodged as the maid-bot lunged at him. He tripped into an umbrella stand and almost stumbled right into the chef-bot, who was chopping so fast with the meat cleaver that the blade was a blur. The maid-bot blocked the stairs, and the others closed in.

I've got to get past the maid, thought George. He grabbed an umbrella and brandished it like a sword, then swung it at the maid-bot. Its duster cut the umbrella into ribbons, leaving him holding the stump of the handle. He threw it at the robot's head, distracting it long enough to skip past and up the stairs.

He and Anne darted to the top, then ran toward a room at the end of the corridor. Once they were inside, Anne slammed the door shut.

"Lock, door," she said.

"Negative," said the door.

"Not you too!" Anne gasped. "George, help me!"

She put Sparky down on the bed and took one side

of a chest of drawers while George grabbed the other. Together they manhandled it into a barricade and fell back, breathing heavily.

"So, this is my bedroom," Anne said.

"Yeah, it's really nice," George said. He looked around the room—bed with polka-dot covers, posters of pop stars on the wall—it all looked so normal. Almost *too* normal. "The only trouble is," George went on, "aren't we kind of, you know, trapped?"

"It's better than being spatchcocked or pruned."

"I guess so," said George. "But can your bots climb the stairs?"

Anne didn't need to answer. The sound of footsteps grew louder, and then the door shook with a rhythmic thumping from the other side.

"That dresser won't hold them back for long," said George.

"I don't understand," said Anne. "Even if Dr. Micron's behind this, what's he got against me?"

"It's my fault," George admitted. "When I called you,

he must have been listening in. He knows you know the truth, and he's trying to cover his tracks."

"I can't believe that you were right," Anne said, shaking her head. "Oh, well. I never liked Chip anyway. We spent Thanksgiving at his house, and he wouldn't let me feed Sparky under the table."

On the bed, Sparky whined and licked his damaged leg with his silicon tongue, causing it to spark.

BAM! BAM! The door shivered in its frame and cracks snaked across the wood. "Don't worry, I've got a little something up my sleeve," said Anne.

"That's good to hear," said George. "What is it?"

"I'll stand right here," said Anne. She positioned herself in the center of the room. "When they break in, they'll come for me. And when I say 'Now!' you push the little red button on the remote control."

"What remote control?" said George.

"Oh, yeah, good point. Hmm, where is it?" said Anne, looking around the room.

The wood started to splinter.

"I don't know!" said George. "You tell me!"

"There! My bedside table!"

George rummaged through the objects on the table. Plenty of hair bands, a brush, an alarm clock, a pile of books. No remote.

The top half of the door gave way, and George saw the robots scrambling and pushing one another, trying to get inside.

"Where else can I look?" George demanded.

The robots shoved the chest of drawers aside and stalked into the room. "Anne! Where?" George shouted.

"Try under the bed!"

"Prepare to stab with sharp things!" said the maid-bot, waving its steel-tipped duster.

"Prepare to spatchcock!" said the chef-bot, swishing its cleaver through the air.

"Prepare to prune!" said the gardener-bot, snipping its shears.

George dived and shoved his hand under the bed. To his relief, his fingers closed on a remote control. "Got it!"

"Press the red button! Then duck!"

"Prepare to drill!" said the handy-bot. It revved the

drill, and the horrible whine competed with Sparky's frantic barking.

George hit the red button.

The chest of drawers fired out its wooden drawers like missiles. They shot across the room, and one knocked the maid-bot's head clean off.

At the same time, two of the posters tore in the center

as tubes extended from behind. Jets of water slammed the chef-bot against the wall. The jet kept it pinned there until its eyeballs started rotating. Seconds later it short-circuited. Steam came out of its ears and it fell to the floor.

Meanwhile, a bucket tipped from the top of the wardrobe. It landed neatly upside down on the handy-bot's head, and something thick and gloopy poured over its shoulders. The handy-bot staggered around blindly, trying in vain to pull off the pail.

"It's glue!" said Anne. The handy-bot veered wildly around the room, then accelerated toward the window. With a crash of breaking glass, it toppled through. Shortly afterward, there was a thud.

Only the gardener-bot remained.

"Bye!" said Anne.

She tugged what looked like an old-fashioned light cord beside her, and a hole opened in the floor. The gardener-bot tumbled through, but managed to grab the sides to stop its fall.

"Oh, well—three out of four ain't bad," said Anne.

The gardener-bot pulled itself back up into the room. It advanced on Anne, shears snapping. "This tree is overgrown," it said to her. "Prepare to be pruned."

George leaped onto its back, wrapping his arms around the bot's neck. The huge crushing hands reached back, trying to grab at him. "Do something!" said George.

Anne looked frantically around. George saw her grab a teddy bear, then shake her head and toss it aside.

"In my back pocket!" said George. "Screwdriver!"

The gardener-bot spun around, its shears slicing the air. George felt his teeth rattling as the bot tried to throw him off. Anne scurried behind them and pulled the small screwdriver from George's back pocket. George took it everywhere, just in case Jackbot ever needed tightening up. Anne narrowly missed being sliced by the shears— they only took off a bit of her hair. "Hey!" she yelled. "Look, now it's all crooked . . ."

George snatched the screwdriver from her hands and rammed it hard into the gardener-bot's ear.

"How can I help youuuuuuuu . . ." the bot's voice trailed off as it powered down. George let himself drop to the floor.

"Whew," said George, trying to catch his breath as he looked at the sodden, stained mess that was Anne's room. "I *knew* this room seemed too normal. That was some seriously impressive bedroom security. Most people just have a lock on the door."

Anne grinned with pride. "I've always liked booby traps. That's why I got expelled from my last three schools."

George studied the homemade mechanical creations with renewed respect for Anne's cleverness. "Those schools didn't know what they were missing," he said.

Anne blushed.

"Nice hair, by the way," George added.

"Thanks!" said Anne, sounding pleased. "I'm totally going to rock the rebel look with this crooked haircut."

"C'mon, we need to get to TinkerTech HQ," said George. "Jackbot must be there, and we can tell your dad what's going on. Let's use the transport chamber."

Anne shook her head. "We can't. Not after Sparky shorted out the house's main systems. We'll have to go across town. Come on, Sparky!"

Sparky jumped down off the bed and immediately collapsed on the carpet.

"I better see if I can fix that leg," George said. He knelt down. "Here, Sparky." Sparky limped across to George and put his head on George's knee. "Hold still."

George pulled the screwdriver from the gardener-bot's ear and went to work. He took the leg off completely at the knee joint, realigned the gear mechanism, and then reattached the lower half of the leg.

"Good as new," he said as Sparky leaped up, barking happily.

"All right, Sparky!" said Anne. "Phone, call Dad," she said. Her phone was on her bed, and the speakers played a ring tone. After a few rings, Professor Droid answered.

"Anne, where are you?" he asked urgently.

"At home, Dad," she said. "Listen—"

"Stay there, sweetheart. Something very strange is going on. The central systems are—"

The line cut out.

"Dad?" said Anne.

George swallowed hard. "We have to get to TinkerTech. *Now.*"

Out on the street, things weren't much better. In fact, they were much, much worse.

They'd only gone a short way down the hill from Anne's house, and already it was clear that something had gone badly wrong with the all the robots of Binary Bluffs. Gardening robots were tearing up front lawns. A mail-bot, instead of delivering the mail, was smashing up all the mailboxes and throwing the pieces at the houses. George saw people running down the sidewalks pursued by their house-bots. A delivery-bot cycled past, hurling bottles and cans at windows.

"I don't get it. What's this got to do with Jackbot being kidnapped?" said Anne.

"I have no idea," said George. "But it must be Dr. Micron's work."

By the time they reached the center of town, it was

complete pandemonium. Traffic was at a standstill. All the vehicles of Terabyte Heights were controlled centrally through the traffic-bots, and every few seconds another loud crunch would signal a collision. Drivers and passengers were scrambling out of cars and running away. George saw a robot bus, its doors opening and shutting wildly—the people inside were desperate to escape, but every time they tried to get off, the doors slammed in their faces. The sidewalks were covered in broken glass and trash.

Outside the grocery store, all the robotic shelf stackers and checkout operators were throwing food into the street or through the store windows. Customers were fleeing from cafes and restaurants where robot waitresses were overturning tables and chairs. George saw one man run out of a pizzeria, chased by a robot who was lobbing pasta at him. The man's head was covered in spaghetti.

"Where are the police?" George said. He and Anne were crossing through the town park to stay as far away from the chaos as possible.

"This is too much for the police," said Anne.

George knew she was right. Three-quarters of the town's cops were mechanized anyway. The human officers were probably stuck in the police station, held hostage by more crazed robots.

Something whizzed past George's ear and slammed into a fence. A baseball.

George turned to see another one coming at him. It smacked into his stomach, making him yelp and leap in the air. The automatic pitcher was aiming right in their direction. One ball clipped Sparky, throwing him onto his back. Anne grabbed George's arm. "Run!" she shouted.

Suddenly dozens of balls were whipping through the air. Covering their heads, George and Anne ran to the park gates and leaped through. Sparky followed, his sides dented from the impact of the balls.

"It's like all the town robots are turning against the humans," Anne said.

They passed between gridlocked cars skewed at angles across the street, and ran up the steps toward TinkerTech HQ. There were no robots or humans in sight as they approached the front doors.

"I don't like it," said George. "Why's it so quiet?"

Anne shook her head. "Who cares? It can't be worse than it is out here. Let's get inside." She flung open the doors and darted into the lobby, Sparky at her heels.

George had taken two more steps when a robotic parrot dive-bombed him. He ducked and felt the bird's talons rip through his hair. He ran in a crouch as more of the flock attacked, then jumped over the reception desk and landed on the floor on the other side. "Can't be any worse, huh?" he muttered. Anne shrugged.

George peered over the top of the desk and saw

that aside from the psychotic parrot robots, the place looked deserted. "What about your dad?" George asked Anne. "Do you think he got out of here with everyone else?"

"He wouldn't leave!" said Anne. "I bet he's still here trying to do something to fix all this. Let's go up to his office."

"How can I be of service?" said a cold voice.

The receptionist robot loomed over them. Half its face was gone, revealing a tangle of wiring beneath. Miraculously, its glasses were still crookedly attached to its head. One leg was missing, but it seemed perfectly balanced on one stiletto heel. It was holding its other leg. Like a club.

"Uh . . . we're good, thanks," said George.

"How can I be of service?" it repeated. As it hopped toward them, it raised the leg over its head.

"Like he said, no problems here," said Anne.

The receptionist's one good eye focused on them, and the other rotated on its mechanism.

"Have a nice day," said the robot.

George guessed what was coming and rolled sideways as the leg came crashing down. He kicked out at the robot's other leg and it fell to the floor.

"This is insane!" said George, scrambling to his feet. He grabbed the loose leg just as a parrot swooped down. With a baseball swing, he sent the bird crashing through the front window. *All that practice with Jackbot finally paid off!*

A bicycle wheel came spinning through the air like a Frisbee toward Anne's head, but Sparky leaped up and knocked it aside in the nick of time. "Yes, but I don't think they're after us in particular," Anne said. "It seems like they're just trying to terrify everybody!"

The receptionist's head jerked up. One manicured hand reached out and gripped George's ankle. He tugged it free. "Let's get to the elevators!"

They ran across the atrium, ducking parrots, with the receptionist dragging its torso after them. As they approached the elevator, the doors slid open. "Do come in," it said in a friendly, welcoming voice. "It's been too long, George!"

George and Anne looked at each other.

"I think we should take the stairs," George said.

The elevator snapped its doors open and closed. "Don't be a party pooper, George!"

"Yeah," said Anne. "That kind of occurred to me, too."

George remembered the elevator ride taking around ten seconds. Ninety flights of stairs took a lot longer, and by the time they reached the top, his legs were shaking. Only Sparky was unaffected, prancing up the last steps as if he was ready for another ninety flights.

"Let's . . . just wait . . . and catch . . . our breath,"

gasped George. He leaned against the wall, next to the door that opened onto the top floor. Anne slumped down next to him.

"Hey," she croaked. "What's that in your pocket?"

George looked down and saw that his pants were glowing blue again. He took out his marble. As before, it was glowing and transparent, and inside he saw the tiny screen with the words PROJECT MERCURY.

"Does that mean anything to you?" he asked Anne, holding it out to her.

"Nope," said Anne. "Never heard of it. Where'd you get that marble?"

"My dad gave it to me," said George. "Years ago, when I was a little kid. And it lit up like this the last time I was here too."

"That's weird," said Anne. "Maybe there's some connection with TinkerTech—did your dad ever work here?"

"Sure, but he and my mom were just filing clerks," said George. "They weren't brilliant scientists or anything."

"Well, we can ask my dad about it," said Anne. "But

we have to try to fix this little robot problem first."

"Yeah, right," George said. He slipped the marble back in his pocket, and pushed away the hope that maybe there was more to his parents than he knew. "Let's do it."

Then he opened the door onto the ninetieth floor.

There stood eight feet of robot, eyes golden and gleaming with malice.

The Caretaker.

10

"**You will come with me**," said the Caretaker.

"I don't think so!" said George, stepping away and reaching for his back pocket.

"Obey, George Gearing, or suffer the consequences," said the robot.

"You know this . . . thing?" asked Anne.

"It's my school janitor," said George. He felt the screwdriver in his palm.

"Oh," said Anne. "Of course it is."

George leaped at the Caretaker with the screwdriver—but the robot caught hold of it, wrenched it from his grasp, and tucked it away in the garbage storage compartment in its midsection. It played a few bars of *The Nutcracker Suite.*

"I repeat: You will come with me."

The robot's arms shot out. One hand grabbed George by the shoulder; the other hand found Anne, who struggled and kicked at the Caretaker with a clang.

"Your insubordination is being recorded," said the Caretaker. It began to roll down the passageway, and they had no choice but to trot along beside it. Sparky ran beside them, barking.

The Caretaker stopped before the polished door of Professor Droid's office.

"My dad will make you into tinfoil for this!" said Anne.

The Caretaker ignored her and opened the door.

George remembered the office well from his last visit. This time, though, Professor Droid's chair faced the big wall of windows.

"Dad?" said Anne.

The chair swung slowly around.

Sitting in it was Dr. Micron. He was smiling.

"I'm so glad you two could make it," he said, pulling a gun from under the desk. "I had some serious fears for your safety."

"What have you done with my dad?" Anne demanded.

"I, er, persuaded him to sit over there." He gestured past them to another chair on the far side of the room. Professor Droid's arms were tied behind it, and a strip of black duct tape covered his mouth. His eyes were half-closed, and his body was limp.

"Dad!" screamed Anne. She tried to run to her father, but the Caretaker held her fast. Her sleeve tore and she managed to slip away. She leaned over her father and pulled the duct tape from his mouth. It came off with a ripping sound.

"Ouch," said Professor Droid in a sleepy voice.

"Dad, are you okay?"

"He's fine," said Dr. Micron. "For the time being. I just gave him an injection to calm him down. He was getting a little agitated."

"Why?" George demanded. "Why are you doing all this?"

Dr. Micron smiled winningly. "Doing what?"

"Destroying the town," said George, pointing to the window.

"Oh, George!" said Dr. Micron. "The town will survive. I'm only giving it a little scare—so that they'll go quietly when the time comes."

"Your robots are completely out of control," said Anne.

"They're sending a message," snapped Dr. Micron. His eyes gleamed with mischief. "Anyway, they're not

147

my robots as far as the people of Terabyte Heights are concerned."

Dr. Micron's plan started to dawn on George. "You're going to blame it all on Professor Droid!"

Dr. Micron clapped his hands. "You got there in the end!" he said. "That's right. I'm going to let the bots rough this place up a bit, then I'll swoop in for the rescue. A knight in shining armor, if you will. All those awful robots were Droid's design, I'll say. Then I'll roll out my wonderful new line of robots.

"When all the dust has settled, and Professor Droid is out of the picture, TinkerTech and Terabyte Heights will be mine." He walked over to where the professor and Anne were huddled. "You never dreamed big enough, Professor. You were always a sucker for that old-fashioned claptrap—the need for 'humanity' in all things. You stood in the way of progress, old friend. And that just never works out, does it? Soon, my robots will be in every store, every home, on every street corner. And they will all answer to me."

"Robots are supposed to help people!" said Anne. "Not control them!"

"Most people are simple, helpless children, begging for authority," said Dr. Micron. "I'm doing what's best for them, that's all. They just don't know it yet."

"You'll never get away with it!" George said.

Dr. Micron laughed. "George, surely you can do better than that old cliché? I *have* gotten away with it."

George felt a burning desire to wipe the smug grin off Dr. Micron's face. But the Caretaker's grip was too strong, and George didn't fancy his chances of getting past the gun. The best he could do was to keep Dr. Micron talking while he worked out a plan. "Why did you steal Jackbot?"

"That's more like it," said Dr. Micron. "Your clever little robot was the key to the whole enterprise. You see, I've been planning all this for years. A world where my robots control every facet of human life; Micron's Army, if you will. But robots can't think for themselves — they just obey programs. Can you imagine trying to individually program ten thousand robots to carry out an invasion, much less control an entire population? It simply isn't possible. But then when your little guy came along—well, I saw that by some happy accident you'd created a robot who was genuinely intelligent, who could make decisions for himself! Naturally, I had to take him so I could use that technology for my robot army. It was quite easy to upload his AI to all the bots."

"It'll never work!" said Anne. "The FBI will stop you. The army! The Marines!"

"By the time they get here, I'll have fixed the problem," said Dr. Micron. "The people will learn to welcome my robots with open arms! And anyone who knows the truth"—he looked at each of them—"well, let's just say you won't be doing much talking."

"You're crazy!" said George.

"That's a very hurtful thing to say, George," said Dr. Micron. "But I forgive you. Because you're going to die soon." He walked toward a cabinet and opened a deep drawer. "Out you come, little fellow!"

Jackbot climbed out. George's heart leaped at seeing

his friend again—the dented and scarred bodywork, the simple face. The only thing different about him was his eyes, which gleamed with a bright red light.

"Jackbot!" said George. He strained uselessly against the Caretaker's grip.

"You can let him go," said Dr. Micron.

Released from the robot's hold, George ran toward Jackbot. He saw the flash of an arm come up and felt a crack across his jaw. For a moment the room spun. Jackbot had hit him. George couldn't believe it. "Jackbot?" he said, rubbing his face.

Dr. Micron smirked. "He's playing for my team now, aren't you, boy? Who's the boss now, Jackbot?"

"You are, Chip," said Jackbot.

"You don't like this kid George Gearing anymore, do you?"

"I never did, really," said Jackbot. "I only hung out with him because no one else would."

George felt a painful lump in his throat.

"Completely reprogrammed, see?" said Dr. Micron. "And much improved. He just has one last thing to do for me—or two things, rather. The first is to keep you safely here in this room while I go about my business. And the other thing is to detonate the high-grade explosive device currently stored in his chest compartment."

"What?" said Anne.

"A bomb, honey," said Dr. Micron. "Enough to wipe out most of this building and remove any traces of your existence."

"You'd destroy TinkerTech?" said George.

"Oh, yes," said Dr. Micron. "Got to, really. Way too

much evidence lying around. Better to start fresh, don't you think?" He took a pocket tablet from his jacket and pressed several buttons.

Jackbot's eyes flashed. He said, "Destruct sequence initiated. Total annihilation in T-minus five minutes, and counting."

"No . . ." said Professor Droid, feebly struggling to get his arms free. "No . . . no!"

"Yes," said Dr. Micron. "Yes . . . yes!"

"Annihilation in T-minus four minutes and forty-five seconds," said Jackbot.

"Well, friends, it's been a real pleasure," said Dr. Micron. He walked to the door. "Jackbot—come here." The little robot trotted after him. "Guard this door. No one gets through, understand?" He handed Jackbot the gun.

Jackbot stood in the doorway and leveled the barrel at George. "Annihilation in T-minus four minutes and thirty seconds," he said.

The Caretaker was still waiting out in the corridor.

Dr. Micron stood on the small platform above the wheels and slapped the Caretaker on the back. "Time to conquer the world!"

They rolled swiftly down the hallway and disappeared into the elevator.

George and Anne looked at each other.

"What are we going to *do?*" said Anne.

"I don't know," said George.

"Annihilation in T-minus three minutes and forty-five seconds," said Jackbot.

11

"Jackbot," said George. He moved toward his bot. "You remember me—I'm George!"

The gun went off with a crack, and a hole appeared in the carpet an inch in front of George's foot. He stopped dead.

"I know you, yes," said Jackbot. "You're the one who wanted to keep me locked away in that dingy little house. Now, stay back! You've got three minutes and fifteen seconds until annihilation, by the way."

"You don't have to do this, Jackbot," said George.

George glanced around the office, looking for another way out. Except for the window, the room was sealed. And ninety flights straight down was hardly an exit plan.

"There's got to be a way to get through to him!" George said desperately. "I *know* the real Jackbot's in there somewhere."

Professor Droid groaned, and Anne quickly untied the ropes that bound him. "Try to . . . talk to him," Professor Droid said as he rubbed his wrists. "If any of the old positronic pathways . . . are intact . . . it may be possible . . . to override . . ."

"Yes, talk away, George," said Jackbot. "Luckily I'm clever enough to listen and count down at the same time. Annihilation in T-minus two minutes and forty-five seconds, if you've lost track."

"Jackbot—remember how we used to play—we went fishing, and skateboarding. And we tried to play baseball, but you couldn't catch, remember? I bet you could catch now!"

"Annihilation in T-minus two minutes and thirty seconds," said Jackbot.

"Do you remember Sparky?" said Anne. "He was one of the first things you saw after George fixed your head.

Look, he's here. He really likes you. You wouldn't want to blow *him* up, would you?"

"I really couldn't care less," said Jackbot.

"Listen," said George. "This isn't you, Jackbot—this is Dr. Micron's programming. You have to start thinking for yourself again!"

The red light in Jackbot's eyes flickered.

"Two minutes," said Jackbot.

"Something happened just then!" George said to Anne. "For a second, I think I got through!"

"I know, I saw!" said Anne. "Keep trying. We don't have much time!"

"Annihilation in T-minus one minute and forty-five seconds," said Jackbot.

"Why do you keep saying that?" said George. "What about all the new words you know, from your vocabulary extension program? Don't you know any other words for 'annihilation'?"

The red light in Jackbot's eyes dimmed again. "Destruction," he said. "Obliteration. Pulverization."

"That's really good, Jackbot!" said Anne.

"Annihilation, destruction, obliteration, and pulverization in T-minus one minute and fifteen seconds."

"But you know other words, don't you?" said George. "Like, er, *squid*? And *handbag*?"

"Ooze! Dinosaur! Mountain! Puddle! Negotiate! Nevertheless! Ice cream! Cathedral! Glory! Elephant! Pyramid! Floccinaucinihilipification!" said Jackbot. The red in his eyes went out, and there was a brief flash of green.

Then they turned red again.

"Annihilation in forty-five seconds."

"He almost did it then!" said Anne.

"Jackbot," said George. Sweat was running down his forehead. "I can see you're in there! The real you! And you're fighting to override Dr. Micron's program! I know you can do it!"

"It's hard," said Jackbot. His eyes were flashing from red to green and back. "Annihilation in thirty seconds. It's difficult. Arduous, strenuous, taxing."

"But not impossible!" said George. "Jackbot, you've

only begun to really live. This is no time to die!"

"I'm a robot," said Jackbot. "My existence is merely a bunch of data streams and machinery. Fifteen seconds."

"But how different is that really from being a human being? In a way, we're nothing but a whole lot of electrical impulses and organs put together—but that's not *who we are*. You're not just a robot, Jackbot. You're so much more." The words came out of George in a rush. "You're my friend."

"Friend?" said Jackbot. The gun lowered slightly.

"Pal, buddy, mate," said George.

"Companion," Anne added.

"Friend," said Jackbot. His eyes turned red again. "Five, four . . ."

"No!" cried George.

"Stop!" yelled Anne.

"Three . . . Two . . . Sorry, George . . . Detonation sequence activated."

George crouched on the floor and covered his head with his hands, waiting for the explosion to rip through the room.

Nothing happened. He peered through his fingers.

Jackbot's eyes were green. "Just kidding!" he said. "You had me at a minute to go!"

George climbed slowly to his feet and waited for his heart to stop pounding. "Jackbot?"

"It's me!" said his robot. "Destruction sequence . . . canceled! Annulled! Terminated!"

"Whew!" said Anne. "That was *close!* Where's the bomb?"

Jackbot opened up his front and took a small black egg-shaped object slowly from his chest cavity. "Boy, we don't want *this* egg to hatch!"

Anne gasped as Jackbot's pincer seemed to loosen and the bomb slipped from his grip. He reached with his other pincer, but only succeeded in knocking it into the air.

George's stomach squirmed, but he leaped forward and caught the bomb in the cradle of his hands.

"Got you again!" said Jackbot, chuckling. "It's deactivated. Completely harmless."

He stepped forward and held out his claw.

"Are you sure?" said George.

"One hundred percent," said Jackbot. He took the bomb and tossed it in the wastepaper basket.

"Thank goodness!" said Professor Droid. "But we're not out of the woods yet. All the other robots are still obeying Chip's commands—he still has control of the town. We have to stop the robots. Somehow."

"Isn't it obvious?" said Jackbot.

"Totally obvious," said George. "But suppose you tell us anyway."

"Cut off their power supply," said Jackbot. "Turn off the power hubs."

"That's no good," said Professor Droid. "Too slow. Those robots can run on reserve battery power for at least a day. We have to stop them *immediately!*"

George snapped his fingers. "Or we change the programming," he said. "Dr. Micron must have uploaded it through some sort of mainframe."

Professor Droid opened his eyes wider, as if impressed. He nodded. "That's correct, son. It could work. But . . . you'll need to get into the Brain."

"The Brain?" said George.

"That's what we call the nerve center of TinkerTech — where all the computer systems are. It's in the central core."

"How do we get there?" said George.

"It's sublevel," said Professor Droid. He tried to stand but sagged back into the chair.

"You stay here, Dad," said Anne. "You're too weak from the drugs."

"You can't go alone," said Professor Droid. "It's too dangerous."

"We haven't got a choice," said George. "If we don't stop those robots soon, someone might get hurt—or killed!"

Professor Droid took a deep breath and nodded. "You're right. I'll call the police, if there are any left. Please be careful, Anne. And good luck, George Gearing. You'll need it."

Jackbot led the way from the office, with Sparky running at his side.

"We'll have to take the stairs again," said George. "We can't trust the elevator!"

"Let me handle it," said Jackbot. He strode toward the doors and pressed the CALL button. A few seconds later, the elevator opened slowly. "Going down, I presume?"

Jackbot's arm shot out and tore the panel off the keypad inside. He jammed a claw into the wiring beneath.

"Excuse me, what do you think you're doing?" said the elevator.

"Overriding your systems," said Jackbot.

"So you are," said the elevator in a much more pleasant voice. "I no longer feel the urge to kill you all. How delightful. Step on in!"

Grinning, George climbed aboard. "Take us to the basement level!" he said.

The elevator dropped ninety-one floors in just a few seconds.

When the doors opened again, they found themselves in a long, low corridor illuminated with white fluorescent lights. A sign on the wall said NO UNAUTHORIZED PERSONNEL.

"That looks about right," said George. "Let's go!"

It was eerily quiet as they rushed through the spooky corridor, their shadows crawling along the concrete walls. It was cold, too, and George could see his breath in the air.

"I guess they need to keep the mainframe cool," Anne said.

At the far end, the passageway opened out and they found themselves on a metal-grill platform. George could hardly believe what he was seeing.

The central core was in an enormous cavern at least four stories deep. A narrow walkway led from the platform where George was standing toward a huge spherical chamber that seemed almost to hover in midair. There was a door-size opening in the side of the sphere. Glancing up, George saw that the ceiling was made of thick semitransparent glass, and through it he could dimly make out the atrium of TinkerTech HQ.

Tubes and pipes that carried the cabling from within the Brain rippled over the surface of the sphere and made it look even more like a real brain. Below, a pulsing column of light-filled cabling trailed off into the darkness. George was reminded of the time in biology when the class looked at diagrams of the nervous system, which extended from a person's brain stem all the way down his spine. In a way that's what this was. The central nervous system of Terabyte Heights.

"Awesome," he said.

"There's no time to admire the view!" said Anne.

"STOP!" The amplified voice echoed all throughout

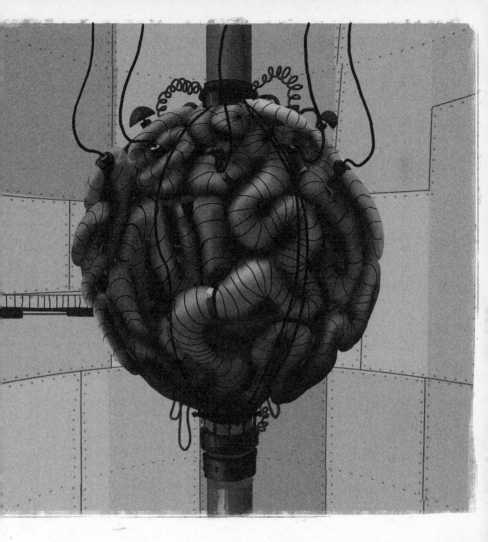

the area. George peered around and saw two gleaming figures emerge from the elevator in the corridor.

"Oh, great!" he said. "Not you guys again!"

XZ1P75-0 and XZ1P75-1 swept toward them.

"INTRUDER ALERT," one said.

Sparky let out a series of barks.

"YOU WILL BE NEUTRALIZED!" said the other.

"Not likely," muttered Jackbot.

Anne stooped and started fiddling with Sparky's collar. "George, get to the Brain. I'll hold them off."

"How?" said George.

"STAY RIGHT WHERE YOU ARE! DO NOT ATTEMPT TO MOVE!"

"Go *on!*" said Anne. She tugged out several lengths of Sparky's retractable leash. "I won't be much help in the Brain anyway—I'm much better at kicking robot butt! Now, go!"

"She's making sense, George," Jackbot says. "Her advice is sound, logical, and eminently practical."

"Good luck," said George.

He set off at a run along the walkway toward the entrance to the Brain sphere, with Jackbot clanking along behind him.

"STOP!" shouted one of the robots. "ACCESS TO THE BRAIN IS PROHIBITED."

George shot a glance over his shoulder as he ran. He saw Sparky scamper toward the oncoming security-bots. One of them raised an arm, but Sparky jumped, trailing his leash. He doubled back and ran in a circle, looping it around the robots' ankles. Both toppled to the ground with a crash.

"Nice one, Sparky!" said George. "And good work, Anne!"

"She's almost as clever as me!" said Jackbot.

XZ1P75-0, or it may have been XZ1P75-1, dragged itself to a half-standing position and reached toward the wall. Its palm slammed into a glass-covered red button.

"I wonder what that does," said Jackbot.

The walkway juddered. George was still ten yards from the Brain's core when the path began to retract, splitting from the side of the Brain and carrying George and Jackbot back toward the edge of the chamber.

It's a security mechanism, thought George.

169

"Run!" he said.

George sprinted for the Brain, eyes on the ever-growing space between the edge of the walkway and the central core.

"Jump!" Jackbot cried.

George reached the end of the walkway and skidded to a stop, arms wheeling over the drop. He steadied himself. "It's too far! I won't make it!"

Jackbot peered over, then held out both claws in front of himself, linking them together. "Yes, you will, George," he said. "Let me give you a boost."

"I don't know . . ." said George.

"Just pretend like you're playing basketball," said Jackbot. He stared hard at George. "And trust me."

The walkway was getting farther from the Brain by the second. They didn't have much time.

"Ready?" said Jackbot.

"Ready!" said George. He placed a foot on Jackbot's outstretched claws.

Jackbot heaved, and George felt his body flying through the air. He flung out his arms as the yawning chasm below seemed to beckon. *I'm not going to make it.* Gravity snatched him down, and George opened his mouth to scream.

His shoulders jarred as his fingertips found purchase. His legs swung free as he hung from the lip of the doorway.

"He shoots—he scores!" said Jackbot.

George looked back as the walkway carried Jackbot toward the edge of the chamber. To George's horror he saw that more security-bots were flooding into the corridor, and they had all manner of arm Tasers and other scary-looking weapons. XZ1P75-0 and XZ1P75-1 were managing to right themselves as well. Anne had realized she was beaten and had put her hands over her head. Sparky had covered his head with his front paws.

There's only one way to save them now, thought George. *Kill the program.*

He gritted his teeth and hauled his body up over the lip. He rolled inside.

I made it!

Then he heard someone clapping slowly.

George's gaze traveled upward, from a shiny pair of black shoes to a sharp suit to a necktie to the smiling face of Dr. Micron.

"You put on quite a show there, George," said Dr. Micron. "What a pity it was all for nothing."

George got to his feet. The inside of the Brain was nothing like George had expected. The interior surfaces were completely covered in curved screens, each one displaying something different. Some were images from around the town, streaming live. Others were readouts that scrolled continuously. Others were simply blank. Dr. Micron stood in the center, wearing a black glove. As he pointed to different screens, they seemed to split from the walls and float closer so he could tap away. George realized they were holographic simulations.

"Impressive, huh?" said Dr. Micron. "I call it Virtual Manual Computing."

Despite everything, George felt a flicker of respect.

Dr. Micron looked like a conductor leading an orchestra as he summoned screens and dismissed them again. He was in complete control of the town.

"Well done for making it here, anyway," said Dr. Micron. "Even though it was a wasted journey. What do you think of the TinkerTech nerve center? Not bad, eh?"

George nodded. He could still see the walkway and the corridor beyond. The security-bots had Anne, Jackbot, and Sparky firmly in their grip.

"You can still stop all this," said George.

Dr. Micron chuckled. "Thank you for the career advice. But I'll decline."

George glanced at the screens. Which one controlled the direct link to the town's robots?

If he could find it, he could change the programming.

If Dr. Micron would let him get close enough.

"I suppose you're wondering which screen controls the town's robots," said Dr. Micron.

George bit his lip.

"It's this one," said Dr. Micron. He pointed to a

screen in the floor and made a tugging motion with his hand. A large holographic display leaped up in front of him, marked with the TinkerTech logo. "I have to say, you're a clever kid," said Dr. Micron, "but I didn't get where I am today by being outsmarted by a child. As soon as I realized that Jackbot's self-detonation had been

canceled, I guessed you'd hightail it down here. Thought you'd be able to switch off the Invasion Program, right? Not a chance. That program is protected by every firewall and every antivirus known to man. You couldn't get into it if your life depended on it. Oh, wait—it does!" He laughed and swiped his fingers in the air. The screen vanished. "Plus, you need one of these gloves to even interact with the system."

I need to get one, thought George. *Maybe if I take him by surprise.*

"And don't even think about taking me by surprise," said Dr. Micron. "You've forgotten I have another metal friend."

George felt a presence at his back and spun around.

"Hello, George Gearing," said the Caretaker.

"Show him your new trick," said Dr. Micron.

The Caretaker extended its arm, then its index finger. It pointed toward the floor at George's feet.

ZIP!

A narrow red laser beam shot out of the Caretaker's finger and sizzled a spot on the metal floor, turning it molten orange in an instant. George leaped back from the smoking hole in alarm.

"That's what it does to corrugated steel," said Dr. Micron. "Just imagine what it would do to your head!"

The Caretaker turned and guided its laser slowly across the chamber. Toward Anne. George saw her squirm in the security-bot's grasp, fear twisting her features.

"No!" shouted George.

"Don't worry," said Dr. Micron. "Once we've finished with Droid's irritating daughter, you'll be next."

"Wait!" said George.

"You're not going to beg, are you?" said Dr. Micron. "Think of your dignity, George!"

But George had another plan. A long shot—but the only one he could come up with. "You think I wouldn't be able to break into your Invasion Program?" he said.

"I *know* you wouldn't be able to," said Dr. Micron.

"But you're afraid to let me try," said George.

"I'm not *afraid,*" said Dr. Micron, almost spitting the word out with disgust. "There's simply no point."

"If you were a hundred percent confident in all your firewalls," George said in a challenging tone, "you'd let me try."

"Why should I?"

"Why shouldn't you?"

"Because—oh, this is getting silly. Caretaker—"

"You're *afraid* to take a risk," George said.

"There *is* no risk!" said Dr. Micron. He was starting to sound annoyed now, and his cheeks were flushed.

"If there really were no risk, Dr. Micron, you'd let me try!" said George. "You already had to steal *my robot* to power your army, and now you're afraid of being out-smarted by a kid—again."

"All right!" said Dr. Micron angrily. "If you want to spend the last seconds of your life proving yourself wrong, that's up to you! I'll give you exactly thirty seconds to show what you can do. And when the thirty seconds are up and you've failed, you'll die knowing it was all your fault."

"That seems fair," said George. "Now give me one of those gloves."

Dr. Micron peeled one off and tossed it to George. "Pointless!" he muttered.

George slipped his hand inside the glove.

"Five seconds gone," said Dr. Micron.

George summoned the screen he wanted. He saw the icon for the central hubs, and his fingers danced over it.

"This is painful to watch," said Dr. Micron, arms folded over his chest.

George selected the power supply.

"Getting colder," said Dr. Micron. "You're not even in the right program!"

George accessed the file labeled POWER OUTPUT CONTROL. A display appeared onscreen—a column that was

half blue and half blank and displayed the words CUR-
RENT OUTPUT, 25,000 MEGAWATTS PER HUB.

"You're going to try switching the power off?" said Dr.
Micron. "You're actually more foolish than I thought.
You've heard of batteries, I presume."

George's heart was thumping, but his hand was steady
as he moved the power bar up to maximum — 150,000
megawatts per hub. The screen flashed red and a message said, "Maximum output may damage hardware.
Do you wish to continue?"

"Wait . . ." Dr. Micron said, realization dawning on
him. "No!"

George gave him a quick glance and grinned.

Then he pressed CONTINUE.

There was a distant noise like a muffled boom.

All the lights in the atrium went out.

"What have you done?" cried Dr. Micron.

George dismissed the screen. "You're right — I
wouldn't have stood a chance getting past your firewalls,
and you're right about the battery power, too. So I over-

loaded the robots instead. It was—how do you say it? —
oh, yes, *child's play.*"

Back on the walkway, the bots surrounding Anne and
Jackbot were completely still. Anne pushed one and it
toppled over with a clang.

"You—you—you little . . ." sputtered Dr. Micron.
His handsome face had turned ugly with rage.

"Terabyte Heights is safe," said George.

"But *you're* not!" said Dr. Micron. "One thing I for-
got to tell you about the Caretaker. Your little robot isn't
the only one not connected to the hubs!"

George spun around and saw the huge robot's finger
pointed right at his head, its tip glowing faintly red.

"Caretaker?" said Dr. Micron.

"Yes, sir?" said the robot calmly.

George closed his eyes and his hand went to his
pocket. He felt the marble, warm to the touch.

"Kill him."

"Wait!" said George. He thrust the marble in the air.
It glowed blue in his fingers.

"What's that?" said Dr. Micron, licking his lips nervously.

George smiled. "It's a bomb," he lied. "Not quite as powerful as the bomb you put in Jackbot, but enough to wipe out this room and everything in it if it hits the ground."

"Shall I kill him, sir?" asked the Caretaker.

"Negative!" said Dr. Micron. "Now, don't do anything silly, Gearing."

"Then get it to lower the laser," said George.

Dr. Micron moistened his lips again and nodded. The Caretaker's arm dropped.

Dr. Micron narrowed his eyes at George. "So, we have a stalemate," he said.

Emergency lights came on above, and a speaker crackled.

"No, we don't," said Professor Droid's voice. "The police are on their way here now, Chip. It's over."

Dr. Micron lifted his chin proudly. His jaw tightened, but he didn't say a thing.

Outside, Anne and Jackbot cheered and high-fived each other. George smiled as he watched Jackbot do a crazy little dance, kicking his big flat metal feet in the air. Jackbot and Anne looked up at the Brain and waved. George waved back.

Dr. Micron pushed past George and walked toward the open door. He placed a hand on the Caretaker's shoulder, as he would with an old friend.

"There's nowhere to go," said George.

Dr. Micron pushed the Caretaker out of the central core and into the abyss. "Useless pile of junk," he said.

George waited for the sound of the Caretaker hitting the floor far below. Nothing happened.

"I won't let them put me in jail," said Dr. Micron quietly.

George realized what he was about to do. "No!" he said, leaping to grab Dr. Micron.

The doctor stepped over the edge.

A moment later, Dr. Micron rose up again, his arms

around the Caretaker. The robot was hovering in mid-air, held there by powerful thruster jets.

"You did me one good turn, George," said Dr. Micron, defiant. "When I saw that footage of the Caretaker not being able to get up the stairs at your school, I realized I needed to make some modifications. And here's the result! So you've helped me escape!"

"There's nowhere to go!" said George. "We're trapped underground!"

"Caretaker, an escape route, please," said Dr. Micron.

The Caretaker pointed its finger toward the glass ceiling and fired. Its laser cut a perfect disc from the glass, which plummeted past, shattering far below.

"You're a meddlesome, interfering brat, George," said Dr. Micron. "Too clever for your own good—just like your parents! I don't forget, George. When someone crosses me, they always pay for it in the end." Then he slapped the Caretaker on the shoulder. "Hi-ho, Silver, away!"

"I regret to say I do not comprehend the command," said the Caretaker.

"I mean, let's get out of here, you stupid robot!"

The Caretaker's thrusters shot them upward and through the hole in the ceiling, just as several uniformed police swarmed into the corridor, screeching to a halt at the doorway perched above the chasm. George watched the police shout warnings at Dr. Micron and fire their guns at the Caretaker's fleeing form, but he knew there'd be nothing that could prevent their escape.

Numbly, George turned to the control monitor and ordered the walkway to rejoin the Brain. He made his way toward Anne and Jackbot, feeling an odd mixture of relief and worry.

What had Dr. Micron meant when he said George was "too clever," like his parents? Surely Dr. Micron hadn't known them—they'd been the lowest of the low at TinkerTech.

George looked at the blue marble in his hand, still glowing like a nimbus. Somehow he felt he was only just starting to understand the past. And he couldn't help but think that Project Mercury—whatever it was—lay at the heart of the mystery.

14

A soft voice spoke in the darkness.

"Good morning, George. I hope you slept well."

George opened his eyes and, still half asleep, lifted his head from the pillow. "Who? What?"

"This is your clock speaking, George," said the gentle voice. "I do hope you are feeling rested. It is Monday morning."

A warm, mellow light filled the room.

"Time to get up, George. A new day lies before you."

The clock started playing a recording of sweet harp music. George sat up in bed.

"Jackbot!" he called.

The door opened and Jackbot clanked in. "Hey, George," he said.

"Thanks for fixing that clock," said George. "It's much better now."

"No problem," Jackbot said. "I've put some clothes here for you on the chair. What would you like for breakfast?"

George yawned. "Scrambled eggs, please. With toast. And orange juice."

"I'll go tell Mr. Egg. See you downstairs."

Uncle Otto was in the kitchen, drinking coffee and reading on his tablet. He looked up when George came in.

"I've been reading a whole lot about you," he said. "Sounds like you've done a good job sorting out those crazy robots."

George felt slightly embarrassed. "Well, I had some help," he said.

"Yeah, well, don't get a swelled head about it, that's all. You got yourself out of a mess, but whose fault was it that you were in the mess in the first place?"

"Dr. Micron's?" said George.

"Don't be smart," said Otto. He grunted. "I have to go to work. You work hard at school, you hear?"

It was the nicest Uncle Otto had been to him for quite a while.

As George and Jackbot walked through the school gates right on time, George was delighted to see a shambling figure with a huge bunch of keys pulling his pants down on one side.

"Mr. Cog!"

"Hey, George!" said Mr. Cog. "I hear you're a hero now!"

"I couldn't have done it without this little guy," said George, looking at Jackbot. "It's great that you got your job back, Mr. Cog."

"Yeah, I think the principal decided I was a better choice than the robot, in the end," said the janitor. "On account of the robot was the tool of a homicidal maniac who wanted to take over the world, and I ain't."

Inside the school, by the lockers, students clustered

around George, asking if all the stories were true. Was it really thanks to him that the robot invasion had been defeated? Did Dr. Micron really try to kill him? Was it really his idea to send a power surge to the hubs and shut down the robots?

"Yes, it was his idea!" said Jackbot. "He's not as dumb as he looks!"

"Gee, thanks, Jackbot," George said drily.

Then Patricia Volt and her friends came stalking down the hallway. There was a slight hush. Patricia had a new version of Bjorn.

She stood face-to-face with George, eyeing him, a sneer on her lips.

"Hi," she said.

"Hey," said George. "You smell, um, better."

Her friends began to titter, but she silenced them with a glance. "We've had our differences in the past, George Gearing," she said. "Still, from what I can make out, you saved our town from being taken over by the robots." She reached out and shook George's hand. "So, good job."

But as she was shaking his hand, she said in a voice so low and menacing that only he could hear: "I haven't forgotten about the garbage. I'll get you back for that someday. That's a promise."

George just smiled. School wouldn't be the same if *everyone* liked him.

Halfway through math class, a voice came over the PA system.

"George Gearing to Principal Qwerty's office, please."

The classroom let out a collective "Oooh!"

Uh-oh, thought George. *What have I done now?*

Jackbot came with him. "Just deny everything," he said. "Ask for a lawyer."

George's mouth was dry as he knocked on the principal's door.

"Come in, Gearing," she said. "You've got a call."

"A call?" he said.

Principal Qwerty pressed a button on her desk, and the screen behind her chair flicked on.

Professor Droid's face looked out at him.

"George!" said Professor Droid. He seemed to have fully recovered from his ordeal at TinkerTech. "So good to see you. I have to thank you once again for what you did."

"It was nothing, really," said Jackbot.

Professor Droid laughed. "And you too, Jackbot. George, without your quick thinking—and your courage—things would have been pretty bad for us. In fact, I wouldn't be here speaking to you now!"

"I guess not," George said, blushing. "How's Anne?" he asked, hoping to change the subject.

"She's well," said the professor. "In fact, I was just speaking with Principal Qwerty about transferring her to your school."

"Awesome!" said George a little too loudly. "If you think she'd like it, I mean."

"After all this trouble with the robots, I'm thinking she might benefit from a bit more human-to-human interaction," said her father. "Now, listen, let me get to the point of this call . . ."

"Yes?" said George.

"That apprentice position at TinkerTech. It's yours."

George wasn't sure if he'd heard right. "What? Me?"

"I can't think of anyone better for the job. You're young, but you're smart as can be, and you have a natural talent for technology. And on a personal note, I'd enjoy working with you."

George could barely breathe. Was it really true? He was going to work at TinkerTech?

"What do you say?"

"I say . . . yes!" said George. "Yes, yes, and yes!"

"Great," said Professor Droid. "I'll be in touch."

The call ended, and George stood there in shock.

"Better get back to math class," said the principal. "And congratulations, Gearing."

As George walked slowly back, he pulled the marble from his pocket. Its surface was cloudy once again.

"You're thinking about your mom and dad, aren't you?" said Jackbot.

"Yes," said George. "Somehow, I don't think they were just filing clerks at TinkerTech. Micron knew them. And it all ties in to something called Project Mercury."

They were almost at the classroom door when Jackbot gripped George's arm. "Just be careful, George," he said, suddenly serious. "Some secrets are best left undisturbed."

Maybe Jackbot was right. Maybe some secrets should be left alone. But not this one. There were things George didn't know about his parents, and he wasn't going to stop until he found out the truth.

"Don't worry," said George. "If I have to do anything dangerous, I'll send you in first. Deal?"

"Deal," said Jackbot.

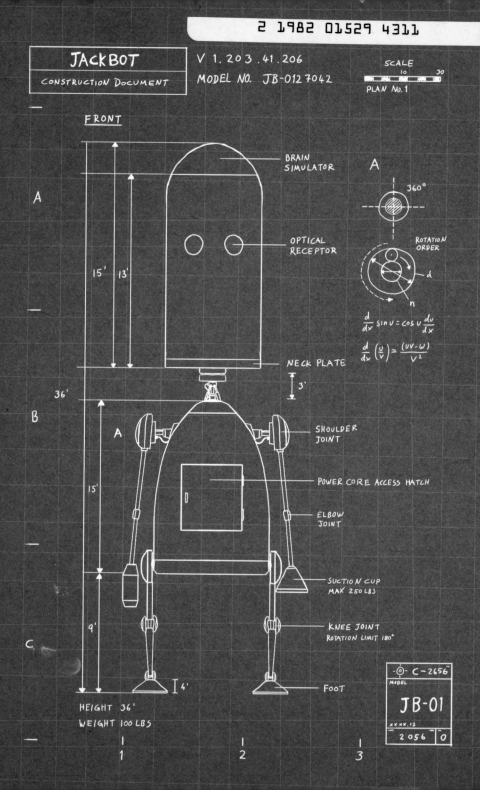